Ballet Friends

Toe-tally Fabulous
#1

Kitty Michaels

Ballet Friends Books
An imprint of Poolside Press

ISBN: 1-4392-0019-X
ISBN-13: 978-1-4392-0019-3

Ballet Friends Books
An imprint of Poolside Press

Printed in the U.S.A.
Charleston, S.C.

Visit us on the Web
www.balletfriendsbooks.com

Book One

 the *Ballet Friends* series

#*1* Toe-tally Fabulous

#*2* Join the Club

#*3* Birthday at the Ballet

#*4* Nowhere to Turn

#*5* Waiting in the Wings

#*6* Dance School Divas

#*7* Ballerinas on Broadway

#*8* Pageant Prima

#*9* The Triple Threats

#*10* The Nutcracker Ballet Club

and also . . .

Once Upon a Tutu: Five Ballet Fairy Tales
Starring the Ballet Friends

Visit **www.balletfriendsbooks.com** today!

1

best foot forward

"I got in! I'm gonna dance in Paris! *Yippee!*" Bianca Best sang, twirling around her room with a special letter from Paris in her hand.

Bianca just got invited to the Paris Pirouette program. It was an amazing ballet school for gifted young dancers in beautiful Paris, France.

Bianca was eleven, and had light blonde hair and sky blue eyes. She just finished fifth grade last week. And now she couldn't wait to move to Paris and start school there in September.

"That's right, Bianca bear, but it says in your letter that you need fifty hours of official pre-pointe ballet class before you can go," her mom said, sitting down on Bianca's pink canopy bed.

"Yeah, I just did the math on my calculator. If I go to ballet camp every day for the whole summer, I'll have exactly the right amount of hours. Things couldn't be more perfect!" Bianca figured.

"Oh gumdrops! Your first hour of class starts really soon. Are you all set to go?" her mom asked.

"Yeah, Mom. Check me out!"

Then Bianca twirled around for her mom. She was wearing a light purple leotard that was covered in sparkly pink and purple crystals.

"Look, I'm *toe*-tally fabulous! I can't wait to try on my toe shoes today!" Bianca cheered.

"Maybe you'll change your mind about going to Paris?" her mom hoped, reading the letter.

"I'll miss you too, Mom. But it's only for a year. Wow, I can't believe I'm going to Paris to be a real prima ballerina! It's a really good thing I'm starting pre-pointe today," Bianca said.

"Oh my gosh, I'm so proud of you. Meet you downstairs," her mom said.

"It's time for my lucky bun!" Bianca called, pulling out a secret gold box from under her bed.

Then she unlocked the box with a key she kept under her pillow. Inside, she found ten ballet buns just waiting to be put on her head.

"Eeny meeny miny moe. Catch a tiger by his toe, or toe shoe. He, he!" Bianca giggled, pointing to the biggest bun in the box.

Then she stuck it on top of her own bun, and pinned it down with some bobby pins.

"I'm fabulous! And I'm Bee-on-ca!" she sang, twirling in front of the mirror.

Then she topped off her outfit by placing a real diamond tiara on her head.

"This is gonna be the best summer ever! I can't believe I'm starting *pointe* today!" Bianca cheered.

After a five minute ride in her mom's white Mercedes SUV, Bianca arrived for ballet camp at the Ridgepoint Community Center.

It was a big white mansion on Main Street with pretty rose gardens, a grand ballroom for weddings, and a ballet studio on the top floor.

"Mom, don't I look *toe*-tally fabulous? I *am* learning toe today. Actually, *toe*-day!" Bianca joked, admiring her tiara in the car mirror, and undoing her seatbelt.

"You do look fabulous! You're my ballet star! You're so sparkly today," her mom giggled.

"That's because it's show time!" Bianca cheered, hopping out and carrying a bunch of pink balloons and a box of hot cinnamon buns.

She pranced right into the mansion, and couldn't wait to get the ballet party started.

Then the white SUV drove off, and next to arrive was a blue Volvo wagon with a license plate which read: "BRACES."

"Megan, we're late. Look, Bianca Best already got here. Oh no, I wanted you to walk in together," Mrs. Fields said to her redhead daughter.

Ballet Friends

"Tell Dad. He's like the busiest orthodontist ever. My whole school was sitting in the waiting room. Why can't I just cut in line? I *am* his own kid," Megan joked, flashing a mouth-full of braces with hot pink rubber bands.

"Megan, just run in. And remember, the faster you run, the more calories you burn. And don't forget you have your clogging lesson after ballet."

"*Gosh, can't a girl just get a summer break?*" Megan whined.

"Oh Megan. Just be happy I couldn't get you into that new circus trapeze class," her mom said.

Then Megan let out a big chuckle, and ran to ballet class with her dance bag.

Off went the blue Volvo wagon, and up next was a tan Honda mini-van with classical music bursting out of the windows.

It was the Levin family performing one of their regular violin concerts, right there in their Honda!

The mini-van's sliding door opened, and a small girl named Lexi (short for Alexis) jumped down to the sidewalk. She carried her violin case, and skipped up the steps to the Community Center. Her brown ponytail danced around as she bounced in.

Then suddenly, behind the mini-van, appeared a large white truck with a food counter and menus stuck to the side. It sat there for a couple minutes, filling the air with smoke. Finally, a girl with curly brown hair hopped out of the back of the truck and rolled into the bushes.

It was Kaylee Klutzopolis. Her family owned the popular Ridgepoint Diner. Kaylee took off her cooking apron, tossed it on the ground, and showed off her bright neon orange leotard and bare legs. Then she climbed into the building through a big open window.

Coughing her way through the cloud of smoke from the restaurant truck, was a tomboy named Jessie Garrett. Tall and thin, Jessie was eleven with straight brown hair, blue eyes, and very fair skin with a sunburn on her nose. She dribbled a basketball up to the curb. Then she placed it under her arm and looked blankly up at the Community Center.

"This is it? Looks like the White House," she shrugged, and added, "If it's boring, I'll just shoot some hoops. They gotta have a basket in there."

Then she casually went up the stairs in her blue sneakers, and was the first girl ever to wear jean shorts and sneakers to ballet.

In the meantime, Bianca was busy turning the dance studio's changing room into a ballet party zone. She hung pink balloons from the coat hooks, and set up pink paper plates on top of the cubbies.

"Cool, free food! Got any pizza?" Jessie asked, strutting right up to Bianca.

"Huh? This party's for my ballet class. Sorry, but I think you're in the wrong place," Bianca replied.

"No, I'm not. So where's the pizza?"

Then Bianca gave Jessie a very confused look.

She checked out Jessie's sneakers, jean shorts, black t-shirt, and long brown hair that looked like it hadn't been brushed in days.

Jessie stared right back at her. She saw Bianca's sparkling diamond tiara, perfect ballet bun, and crystal-covered leotard. Then she shrugged and tossed her basketball in the air, and caught it with one hand.

"Um . . ." Bianca started to say.

But just as Bianca was about to tell Jessie there was no pizza and maybe offer her a hot cinnamon bun instead, she was interrupted by a very hungry and over-excited Megan Fields.

"Hi, Bianca! You brought food? *Do I smell Cinnabon?* Wow, you're the best!" Megan panted, dropping her dance bag at the door.

"Well that *is* my name – Bianca Best. But yes, Megan, your nose is correct. Cinnabon anyone?" Bianca offered, opening the big box of treats.

"Don't mind if I do!" Jessie called, reaching for a hot and gooey cinnamon bun right out of Megan's hands, and taking a big bite.

"Hey! That was mine! *Cinnabon stealer!* But really, who are you anyway?" Megan chuckled.

"Yeah, who are you?" Bianca asked.

"I'm new here," Jessie replied.

"Oh cool, a new girl! Welcome to Ridgepoint, Connecticut!" Bianca cheered.

"Ooh, ooh, Bianca! I *looove* your tiara! Wanna share a *barre* in class?" Megan interrupted.

Megan was hoping to finally make friends with Bianca this summer.

"Huh?" Bianca went, still looking at Jessie.

"Ooh, ooh, you wanna share a *barre?* Let's stand together in class, okay?" Megan squealed.

But Megan lost her chance to hear Bianca's answer, when suddenly Bianca's two best friends since pre-school showed up.

They were Jill Bertucci and Courtney Gates. Jill was tall, skinny and blonde, and her sidekick Courtney was short, chubby, and had brown hair.

"Look, Court. It's Meggy Fields! Where's your mommy, *Meggy?* She's always with you," Jill teased, pointing at Megan.

"Ha, ha!" Courtney laughed.

"But she just dropped me off, Jill," Megan muttered.

Then Jill grabbed Bianca to whisper some gossip in her ear.

"Oh boy," Megan sighed, leaning back onto a cubby, but missing it and falling onto little Lexi.

"*Ouchy!*" Lexi cried, and hid inside an empty cubby hole with her violin case.

"Oh no! I'm sorry, kid. I didn't see you there. Here, have a Cinnabon," Megan said, handing Lexi the last cinnamon bun.

"OMG! Is she okay? Megan, what did you do?" Bianca cried, rushing over to Lexi.

"She's fine. I gave her the last Cinnabon. I made up for squishing her," Megan said.

"The last Cinnabon? But I brought enough for the whole class. Megan, how many did you eat?" Bianca demanded.

"Not as much as me," Jessie snorted, wiping tons of frosting off her mouth and onto her sleeve.

"OMG, who are all the new people?" Jill huffed, glancing at Jessie and Lexi.

"Come on, Jill. Be nice. This is my ballet party. Sorry she ate your Cinnabon," Bianca whispered.

"Are you kidding? Do you know how much fat is in one of those? Like I'd ever," Jill grunted.

"Hi guys. Do I smell Cinnabon?" Kaylee said, wandering in and sniffing Lexi's bun.

"Yup, but there's no more," Jessie replied.

Then Kaylee turned to Bianca and giggled.

"Yeah there is! Right there on Bianca's head!" Kaylee cried, pointing at Bianca's big ballet bun.

"OMG! You girls are so silly," Bianca laughed with everyone.

Then they were interrupted by the ballet teacher.

"Hello girls! If you're done with your little party, it's time for class. Come in quickly and start your warm-ups. And little boy, go away! Go home!" Madame Simpson exclaimed at Jessie, shooing her away like a stray dog.

"Where's the boy? I'm no boy. I'm here for ballet," Jessie replied.

"*You are?* Well, um, perhaps you'd like to change before class?" Madame Simpson asked, fussing with the blue scarf on her head.

"Huh? I'm already in my gym clothes," Jessie said, posing with her basketball under her arm.

Madame Simpson shook her head in disbelief. Then she showed the new student into class and waved everyone into the studio.

"Hurry in and take your places at the *barre* and assume first position!" Madame Simpson called, clapping her hands.

Then the small class of sixth grade girls ran to the *barre.* They slid their heels together, and tried to make a straight line with their feet. Then they checked themselves out in the mirror.

But Jessie hung back and didn't have a clue what first position was, so she copied Megan by making a sloppy "V" with her feet.

"Now before we begin our *plies,* I want to welcome you to ballet camp. This is the pre-toe summer workshop. Looks like you're all here at the right time, except for that little girl in the back. Excuse me, honey, Baby Ballet is on Tuesday," their teacher said.

Then everyone turned and stared at little Lexi.

"Um, I'm eleven. I just look six," Lexi said, fluttering her pretty, baby doll lashes.

Lexi was still nibbling on her Cinnabon, and she had some frosting on her nose.

The class broke out in giggles, and Lexi's cheeks turned bright red. Then she looked down at her teeny-tiny ballet slippers.

"Anyhoo class, this summer you'll be learning how to dance in *pointe* shoes. With any luck, you won't need your old ballet slippers much longer," their teacher explained.

"Yes!" Bianca cheered.

"But of course, we'll start out slowly. At the end of each class, you'll get to try on my old *pointe* shoes," their teacher added.

"*Used shoes?* Madame Simpson, I brought my own. They're brand new. See?" Bianca boasted.

Then Bianca pulled out the most fabulous pair of hot pink toe shoes from her white Chanel tote bag. Her toe shoes came all the way from Paris, France, and so did her very fancy dance bag.

"Hot pink *pointe* shoes?" Madame Simpson asked in total surprise.

"Fuschia," Bianca proudly replied.

"*Few-shuh?*" the class gasped.

"Of course. I have to show up on stage, you know," Bianca giggled.

"Well, I'll allow it," her teacher decided, and nodded at her most enthusiastic student.

Then the girls began their warm-ups. Bianca declared herself the Junior Instructor, and led the class in *plies.* Tomboy Jessie still had no clue what to do, and copied everything Megan did – even when Megan did it the wrong way.

2

field trip

Right at the end of class, Madame Simpson made a surprise announcement.

"Class, you have homework," she said.

"But it's summer," Jill blurted, and rudely smacked her gum.

"Well alright, but I guess you don't want to hear about your field trip to the mall," their teacher shrugged.

"Did you say the mall?" Bianca asked, with her face lighting up.

"That's right. Your homework is to go to the mall and practice walking gracefully in front of people. This will get you ready for the stage. And don't forget, you must walk toe-to-heel!"

"Ooh, ooh! The Ridgepoint Mall? They have the *best* food court – McDonald's, Sbarro, Taco Bell, not that I'm allowed to eat there," Megan blurted.

"And don't forget Cinnabon!" Bianca cheered, smiling at Megan.

"That's cool. I could use another," Jessie said.

"Um, I'm still working on mine. Is that okay?" Lexi shyly asked.

Then everyone giggled.

"That's the mall, girls. Oh, and one more thing. You have to go together as a class," their teacher added.

"*Together?*" the girls asked.

"That's right. And you have to go like that," she added, pointing to their ballet leotards, pink tights, and ballet slippers.

"*In our leotards?*" Megan asked.

"*To the mall?*" Jill gasped.

"Right now? But Megan has her clogging class now!" Megan's mom called, rushing into the dance studio with Megan's thick day planner in her hand.

"Oh boy," Megan sighed, hoping Bianca wasn't paying attention.

"Oh Mrs. Fields, can she miss it this one time?" Madame Simpson asked.

"I suppose, but Megan has her Italian opera singing lesson at three that she just can't miss. So I better drive them," Mrs. Fields decided.

"Mom, you're embarrassing me," Megan whined, rolling her eyes and making a miserable face.

But then something suddenly came over Jill and Courtney.

"*Cough, cough,*" Jill faked, nudging Courtney in the side.

"Oh yeah. *Cough, cough,*" Courtney copied.

"Girls, are you feeling okay?" Madame Simpson worried.

"Um, I think we're getting sick. Actually, I know we're getting sick. We can't go to the mall with you," Jill announced.

"Yeah, what Jill thed," Courtney lisped.

"OMG! No, you're not. You're coming to the mall with us," Bianca insisted.

"No, we're not!" Jill argued.

"If we don't leave right now, Megan will never make her opera lesson. Whoever's going, let's go now!" Mrs. Fields urged, heading downstairs.

Then Jill and Courtney grinned, and waved for Bianca to stay back with them.

"OMG, I knew you guys were faking. What's up?" Bianca whispered.

"What's up with you? You'd be seen at the mall with Meggy and Kaylee the klutz? And those weird new girls?" Jill asked back.

"They're not weird. And stop calling Megan and Kaylee names. It's getting old. You know, they've been in ballet with us forever. Why do you have to be so mean to them?" Bianca argued.

"Mean?" Jill gasped.

"What?" Courtney went.

13

"Uh, yeah. Can't you just be nice to them?" Bianca asked.

"Whatever. C'mon Court, let's go to my house," Jill decided, walking out of the studio.

"Yeah, leth go," Courtney nodded.

A few minutes later, the girls piled into Megan's blue Volvo wagon.

"I can't believe Jill and Courtney said they got sick," Bianca complained, as she climbed into the front passenger seat.

"That's fine with me," Megan muttered from the back seat.

"If it wasn't for them holding us up, I could be at Victoria's Secret by now," Bianca figured, fussing with her tiara.

"You wear Victoria's Secret?" Megan gasped.

"Of course, they're my gym class bras. But I get all my fancy ones from Saks Fifth Avenue. Anyway, it looks like some of you could use a bra, too. Um, Jessie is it?" Bianca dared to ask the new girl sitting right behind her.

"Huh?" Jessie went, still thinking about hot cinnamon buns.

"Ooh Bianca, cute leotard. What brand is it, and what size are you now? See Megan, you *can* wear a bra under your leotard," Mrs. Fields announced, climbing into the driver's seat.

"*Mo-om!*" Megan yelled from the back seat.

Then Bianca chuckled.

"Oh Megan," Mrs. Fields sighed, adding, "Hey, are you ready for a big mall walk? You need to walk at least four miles around the mall. Especially since you're missing your Calorie Burning Clogging class. And no eating at the food court. It's bad for your diet."

"Not even Cinnabon?" Bianca asked.

"Especially not Cinnabon – wait a minute, do I smell cinnamon?" Mrs. Fields sniffed.

"Um, I'm sorry. I'm still eating mine," Lexi squeaked.

Then Megan leaned over to smell Lexi's bun.

"Megan, don't even think about it!" her mom called.

"Ugg, I was just smelling it," Megan sighed.

"Wait, I know you," Mrs. Fields said, turning around to look at Lexi.

"You do?" Lexi asked.

"Yes! Weren't you the Concert Master and first chair violin in the Ridgepoint Elementary School orchestra?" Mrs. Fields asked.

"Um, yes. Is that okay?" Lexi replied.

"Well do you have to be so good? You're the reason why Megan got stuck playing the viola last year. She sounded so bad next to you on the violin that the teacher took her out of third violin and made her play the viola."

"*Mo-om!* You're spilling my guts to everyone, including Bianca Best!" Megan shrieked.

Then everyone giggled at Megan.

15

"Oh Megan. It's no secret you stink at violin. At least you're an excellent singer. By the way, Lexi, who's your private violin tutor?" Mrs. Fields asked.

"Can we just get going now?" Megan insisted.

"Don't worry, Megan. If I was in the orchestra, I'd be *tenth* violin!" Bianca joked, turning around and grinning at Megan.

"Really?" Megan giggled.

Then Lexi turned to the tomboy sitting behind Bianca, and said, "Um, who are you again?"

"Jessie. Jessie Garrett. But you can call me Jessie," she replied.

Then Bianca glanced back at Jessie, and giggled.

"Hey guys, where should I sit?" Kaylee asked, still standing outside the car.

"Oh, we almost forgot about you," Mrs. Fields said, and added, "Uh, girls, can you make room for Kaylee in the back?"

"*Mom, there's no room!*" Megan called.

"Of course there's room. Kaylee can sit backwards in the cargo area," Mrs. Fields replied.

"Cool, I can make silly faces at the other cars!" Kaylee cheered.

With everyone finally in the car, Mrs. Fields pulled out of the Community Center's parking lot, and zipped across town to the Ridgepoint Mall.

Ten minutes later, they arrived and Bianca clapped at the sight of the mall.

"*Ooh, they sell gerbils here,*" Kaylee cooed.

"Didn't know that. Didn't care," Megan went.

"Okay, everybody out," Mrs. Fields said.

"Wait, somebody has to hold my hand in the parking lot. It's the rules," Lexi said.

"I'll do it for two bites of your Cinnabon," Jessie quickly replied.

Then Mrs. Fields came around the car holding an overstuffed black duffel bag.

"Oh no! Not my gym bag! I'm just walking around the mall – not running," Megan feared.

"Look, girls. We're not at the dance studio anymore. We're at the mall, so cover up. I'm the mom here and I say you do this assignment wearing sweats and track pants," Mrs. Fields declared.

"Phew!" Megan went.

"But Mrs. Fields, our teacher said to go in our leotards," Bianca insisted.

"Yes, I know dear, but this is for the best."

"Yeah, you want boys to see us in our leotards?" Megan pointed out.

"Exactly. Hurry up, girls. Megan has her opera singing class this afternoon," Mrs. Fields said.

After throwing on some Ridgepoint High School sweatpants, track pants, and a sweatshirt for Lexi that became a dress, the group headed right into Macy's still wearing their ballet slippers.

Once inside, the girls found themselves in the middle of the bra department.

"Hey Bee, this must be your favorite department!" Jessie called.

Bianca laughed and said, "You pegged me! You're good, and you've only known me for like two minutes. Let's go get you some bras!"

"Ah-ight," Jessie nodded, and added, "I guess that's cool."

And just like that, Jessie and Bianca clicked and started browsing through some bras.

"Mom, can we meet you later? *Please?* I'm pretty sure our teacher wants us to practice walking by ourselves. You don't have to chaperone us. *Pleeease?*" Megan begged.

"Hmm. I could get my toenails painted. Well, okay, but I'm putting Bianca in charge," Mrs. Fields decided.

Bianca nodded, and gave a wink to Megan to let her know it was cool.

"Thanks, Mom! Don't worry, and don't hurry either! Really, take your time!" Megan insisted.

"I'll meet you girls back here in exactly two hours. And don't be late," her mom ordered.

"But Mom, we're almost teens! We're supposed to *live* at the mall! *Two hours just isn't enough!*" Megan protested.

"Two hours, be here," Mrs. Fields repeated, and headed off to get her toenails painted.

Just then, Kaylee wandered off in her neon orange leotard and purple sweatpants to a display of plus-size women's underwear.

18

"Snap! What's Kaylee doing? She's more embarrassing than my mom!" Megan cried.

The girls watched as Kaylee reached for the biggest pair of underpants on the table.

"Kaylee, let go of those large underpants this instant," Bianca ordered.

"But I want them," Kaylee whined.

"They're *way* too big for you," Bianca argued. "You can't possibly wear those."

"*But I want them!*" Kaylee repeated.

"Kaylee dear, I didn't want to have to say this, but your underpants protrude out of your leotard," Bianca pointed out.

"Um, yeah, they stick out," Lexi agreed.

"So what?" Kaylee said.

"*So what?* Looks like they're fallin' down your legs," Jessie laughed.

"Oh Jessie, you crack me up!" Bianca laughed, and added, "*Anyhoo,* let's go, girls! Toe-to-heel! Toe-to-heel!"

3

ballerinas on the move

A few minutes later, when the girls left Macy's and entered the crowded mall, they drew some stares and double-takes.

"What? They've never seen ballet class at the mall before?" Bianca joked, leading the group in their very graceful, toe-to-heel mall walk.

"*Beep, beep!*" a little boy went, and ran around them.

"Hey! Ballerinas here!" Jessie called.

Then everyone giggled.

"That's the idea, Jessie. You know, you're really good at toe-to-heel. How much ballet have you taken?" Bianca asked, passing Sears.

"This is my first day," Jessie revealed.

"*It is?* You're such a natural," Bianca said.

"So why are you in ballet?" Megan asked.

"For some reason my dad wants me to be more lady-like," Jessie said, letting out a burp.

"Um, it's my first day, too. Is that okay?" Lexi chimed in.

"Of course, sweetie. What brings you to ballet? You're like the star of the school orchestra," Bianca asked.

"Don't remind my mom!" Megan joked.

"Well, I like the music and it looks pretty," Lexi replied.

"Very good reasons, Jessie and Lexi. Welcome to ballet. It's going to be a very exciting summer. We're gonna learn *pointe,* and have so much fun!" Bianca exclaimed.

"Cool!" everyone went, wandering into Claire's.

"Well, now about *moi.* That's 'me' in French, *mwah.* Anyway, I love ballet and bling, and I love to do my hair. And I'm super excited to start *pointe* and eventually *pas de deux,*" Bianca shared.

"Potty-doo?" Lexi giggled.

"OMG, you're so cute. That's French for partner work," Bianca explained.

"Ooh, ooh! I'll be your partner, Bianca!" Megan burst out, hopping up and down in her slippers.

"That's nice, Megan, but it's boy-girl," Bianca chuckled, and led the group out of Claire's.

Then they all heard a loud growl that sounded like a ferocious beast.

"Oh no, Megan! Was that your stomach?" Bianca giggled in front of the Gap.

"You mean you heard that?" Megan said, blushing.

"Um, yeah. We all did. *Cinnabon anyone?*" Bianca laughed.

"Yeah!" everyone cheered.

"But guys, you forgot. I'm not allowed to eat Cinnabon," Megan reminded them.

"Well, what about back before class?" Bianca asked.

"Jessie ate it. I only got to smell it!" Megan complained.

"Oh, sorry," Jessie shrugged.

"That's okay, as long as I can get a make-up Cinnabon right now?" Megan hinted at Bianca.

"Of course. To the food court, everyone! Don't forget I'm in charge!" Bianca called.

Just when the group got off the escalator and were just a couple feet from the food court, Bianca caught a glance of something, but it wasn't hot cinnamon buns.

Standing in front of Cinnabon were none other than Jill and Courtney. Jill had her nose over Courtney's cinnamon bun and was smelling it, while sipping a fat-free latte.

"O-M-G! It's Jill and Courtney! They're supposed to be home sick! And what are they doing eating our Cinnabons?" Bianca yelled.

At that moment, Jill and Courtney turned around and looked right at Bianca.

"Oh snap! They see us! C'mon guys, let's go!" Megan called, heading back to the escalator.

"No way! If anyone should go, it's them! *We're* supposed to be here," Bianca insisted.

Then Jill waved Bianca over.

"Um, I think she wants you, Bianca," Lexi said.

"Go ahead, Bee. See what they want," Jessie said.

"And bring back my Cinnabon," Megan added.

"Oh fine, but I don't even want to talk to them," Bianca sighed, and headed over to Jill and Courtney.

"Hey Bianca. Why are you still with them? Haven't you walked enough?" Jill asked.

"Yeah, have a Thinnabon with uth," Courtney offered.

"OMG! You guys wouldn't eat *my* Cinnabons!" Bianca complained.

"That's cuz the new girls ate them. Those pigs!" Jill huffed.

"They're not pigs! I was making a ballet party and you dissed me!" Bianca exclaimed.

"No we didn't. We just didn't wanna hang out with those losers," Jill said.

"They're not losers, you two are!" Bianca snapped, and grabbed Courtney's Cinnabon and tossed it into the trash.

"Hey, my Thinnabon!" Courtney yelled.

Then Bianca smiled to herself and joined her new ballet friends.

"Ooh, that was so cool! But did you have to throw the Cinnabon in the trash?" Megan asked.

"Oh Megan, I promise I'll get you a hundred Cinnabons – cuz we're gonna be hanging out all the time!" Bianca declared.

"*We are?*" Megan gasped, almost fainting.

But Megan's perfect BFF moment with Bianca was interrupted by Lexi:

"Um, I think we lost a kid. Is that okay?"

"OMG! It's Kaylee!" Bianca exclaimed. "We're missing Kaylee!"

"Oh snap! My mom's always yelling at me for losing stuff, and now I lost a kid? What am I gonna do?" Megan wailed.

"Eh, don't worry, we'll find her," Jessie said.

"Shoot. We better go look for her now," Megan worried.

"I'm sure she'll turn up. She's wearing a neon orange leotard and purple sweatpants!" Bianca exclaimed.

"I'm gonna get grounded!" Megan cried, throwing a fit in front of Radio Shack.

"Calm down, we'll find her. You are with *moi.* I could walk this mall in my sleep," Bianca boasted.

Racing back to Macy's, the group returned to Kaylee's last known location: the bra department. She was last seen shopping for underwear.

"Here we are, bras and undah-shorts. Bianca's Candy Land!" Jessie announced.

"OMG!" Bianca burst out laughing.

Then Megan got super-jealous and tried to think of something funny to say.

But then Jessie beat her again.

"Hey Bee, do I gotta match my bras with my clothes? And what about my undah-shorts? Do they gotta match, too? That's a lot of work."

"*Your undershorts?*" Bianca repeated, and then replied, "Well, to answer your question, yes! Your underwear must coordinate at all times!"

Then Bianca and Jessie shared a big laugh, and put their arms around their shoulders like BFF's.

"Gees, I'll be spendin' all morning before school matchin' my underwear," Jessie joked.

"Oh Jessie!" Bianca burst out.

Then Bianca hiccuped from laughing so hard.

"I'm wearing Care Bears underwear," Lexi announced out of the blue.

"Oh my God! I'm not sharing about *my* underwear!" Megan shrieked, and rolled her eyes at Lexi.

Then Bianca cracked up so bad, she accidentally let out a surprising burp.

"Good one, Bee! So where's the fittin' room? I'll try some on. I'm game!" Jessie called.

"Jessie, you're not allowed to try them on. You're supposed to buy them in the package," Megan snapped.

"Oh no, Megan. At Saks Fifth Avenue, I order them from behind the counter. I even have them printed with my initials, B.B.," Bianca bragged, still giggling.

"I got a marker at home. I'll print J.G. on them myself," Jessie decided.

"I know! That's it! Kaylee must've locked herself in the fitting room!" Megan decided, "Oh brother, let's go rescue her already."

Then the girls checked the fitting room, and called out Kaylee's name, but nobody answered.

"While we're here," Bianca grinned, "Why don't we try on some bras?"

"Ya think I need one?" Jessie asked.

"For sure," Bianca replied, adding, "And maybe I'll pick up some more gym bras."

"No way. Bianca, don't you have enough bras already?" Megan complained, itching to get out of the bra department.

"Megan, one can *never* have too many bras," Bianca stated.

"See ya!" Megan blurted, and turned around to run out of the fitting room.

"Freeze!" Bianca called, pulling Megan's arm, "I was talking to *you,* Megan."

"Oh snap!" Megan went.

"You could use a bra," Bianca said.

"Gosh, what are you, the Bra Police?" Megan accused.

"I'm just trying to help," Bianca added.

"Well, I don't need one – I'm already wearing Spanx," Megan said, whispering the last part.

"What?" Bianca asked.

"Spanx!" Megan replied louder.

"Oh no," Bianca giggled.

"Oh yes. My mom makes me wear it. I hate it. It's way too tight. But what can I do?"

"Well, maybe I can talk to your mom on the ride home," Bianca offered.

"*Really?* You would do that for me? But it's supposed to be a secret."

"Um, Bianca, do you think I need a bra, too?" Lexi interrupted, also wanting some attention from Bianca.

"Hmm, not yet, Lexi dear. But maybe we can find a nice little cami for you," Bianca expertly noted, and added, "But let me work on Jessie first. She's more in need."

"Oh, I know! We should call you *Bra-inca,*" Megan chuckled.

"Bra-inca? I'd prefer the Bra Police," Bianca joked.

"Hey Bee, how's this?" Jessie asked, coming out of a fitting room, wearing just a pink bra and her jean shorts, with all the bra tags dangling from her underarms.

"Cute bra! Hey Jay, when did you sneak off and go bra shopping?" Bianca giggled.

"Hey, hey! I'm Meg! Call me Meg!" Megan called, jumping up and down.

"You're acting like a dumb little kid," Lexi said, shaking her head at Megan.

"Oh Lexi," Bianca giggled.

"Guys, if you're not gonna call me Meg, then we might as well go find Kaylee," Megan sighed.

"You're right, *Megan.* We'll look for *Kay* after *Bee* pays for my stuff," Jessie said, laughing with Bianca and teasing Megan.

The gang spread out all over Macy's and called out Kaylee's name about a million times. They looked in Makeup, Perfumes, Furniture, Shoes, and Juniors, until finally, Lexi called out:

"I found her! Over here, everybody!"

The girls followed Lexi's voice, and gathered in front of last season's winter coats. It was the quietest part of the store. There were no customers or even sales people around.

Lexi motioned for them to follow her, and parted a rack of winter coats.

It was then everyone saw Kaylee sitting on the floor in a corner. She was playing with a small, tan furry animal crawling in front of her.

"Oh, hi guys! Where's your leotards? I'll tell on you," Kaylee said, looking up at them.

"Like *you're* doing your homework!" Megan snapped.

"I'm wearing my leotard! And look, Harry's walking toe-to-heel!" Kaylee shot back.

"*Harry?*" the girls asked.

"My new gerbil, Harry! Isn't he beautiful?" Kaylee cheered, playing with his tail.

The girls rolled their eyes at each other, and yanked Kaylee off the floor to go meet Megan's mom.

"Wait, I need to get Harry!" Kaylee cried.

"That *thing* is riding in back with you," Bianca declared, and pinched her cute little upturned nose.

And the girls somehow met Megan's mom in Macy's right on-time.

They entered the mall as five ballet classmates, but left as five ballet friends . . . and one gerbil mascot.

4

class act

The next day in ballet, Bianca stood next to her best friend at the *barre* and whispered something in her ear and giggled. But it wasn't Jill or Courtney.

It was Jessie! And she was all glammed up, thanks to the instant makeover Bianca gave her before class in the changing room.

"Oh, is there a new student today?" Madame Simpson asked.

"It's me, Jessie Garrett. I'm wearin' tights!" Jessie announced, and lifted one leg.

Then the whole class stared at Jessie. It was more than just the lip gloss and blush from Bianca, or her new leotard, tights, and ballet slippers that made her look different today.

Jessie was a completely new person – and joined at the hip with Bianca.

"I don't get it?" Megan shrugged.

"Um, what's wrong? Am I no good?" Lexi frowned, standing up straight, with her head at the same height as the *barre.*

"No, I'm talking about them. Since when are *they* best friends? We all went to the mall, didn't we? What's so special about Jessie?" Megan blurted.

But Megan wasn't the only one who noticed.

Jill and Courtney were very annoyed by the new best friends, and did everything they could to let Bianca know.

"Look, they're Bianca Besties! Get it? Bianca Best and her besties!" Jill cried, during warm-ups.

"Yeah, good one!" Courtney laughed.

"Hey, ya makin' fun of me? Don't let my makeup fool you. I'm from the city," Jessie flung back.

"Then go back there!" Jill fired.

"Don't worry about them, Jay. They're mean to everyone they're jealous of," Bianca said.

"*Jealous?*" Jill huffed.

"*No way,*" Courtney also huffed.

But then their teacher said:

"Girls, behave! From now on, you can only talk about ballet. It's my new rule. Anyhoo, let's start by reviewing the basics. When you're at the *barre,* your hand should rest comfortably on it, so that it's just in front of your body. Just like Bianca's doing. If you're not sure, do what Bianca's doing."

"Well I *am* the Junior Instructor," Bianca boasted, and rolled her eyes at Jill and Courtney.

Jill and Courtney rolled their eyes back, and smacked their gum at the same time.

After class resumed, Lexi broke the silence while everyone was practicing first position.

"Um, Megan, is it okay if I ask you a question?" Lexi shyly asked her neighbor at the *barre.*

"Sure, kid. Ask away," Megan replied.

"Um, can I scratch my arm?"

"Why not, kid? You got an itch, scratch it."

Later, while practicing second position, Lexi spoke again:

"Um, Megan, is it okay if I ask you a question?"

"Again? Shoot."

"Um, am I allowed to blow my nose?"

"Yeah, but don't make too much noise."

Then in the middle of third position, Lexi asked:

"Um, Megan, is it okay if I ask you a question?"

"*Another question?* Well, okay."

"Um, where's the potty?"

"You're outta luck, kid. It's locked, and they only open it for weddings."

Then Lexi put her knees together, and did a little dance.

And by fourth position, Lexi loudly asked:

"Um, I got another question!"

"*What?*" Megan went.

"Um, when's my mommy picking me up?"

"Not soon enough!"

By fifth position, Lexi was dancing like a Mexican jumping bean.

"Um, um, um, I gotta ask you another question!" Lexi cried.

"Stop asking!" Megan snapped.

"Oh, okay. I won't ask you if there's even a boys room I can use."

"What? Oh, *eww!*" Megan yelped, accidentally backing into Kaylee.

Then Kaylee the klutz lost her balance, teetered for a moment, then fell onto Megan, who then fell onto Lexi, and the three ballerinas crashed down together on the floor.

"That was fun! Let's do it again!" Kaylee cheered, lying flat on Megan's back.

"Get off me, you klutz!" Megan yelled, squirming to get Kaylee off her.

"OMG, little Lexi! Megan, you crushed her!" Bianca exclaimed, quickly running over to rescue Lexi, who was on the bottom of the pile.

"Bianca, toe-to-heel, toe-to-heel! This isn't a track meet!" their teacher called.

"Lexi! Are you okay? Say *arabesque* if you're okay!" Bianca cried, hovering over Lexi.

"Yeah, tiny tot, say airy-bess!" Jessie called.

"Airy what? I don't know what that is. Um, that was sort of fun, but don't do it again, Megan!" Lexi barked, getting up.

"What? It's all Kaylee's fault!" Megan insisted, pointing at Kaylee.

"Madame Simpson, can Lexi stand next to me and Jessie? Megan might fall on her again," Bianca asked, holding hands with Lexi.

"But Bianca, I told you it wasn't me! It was Kaylee!" Megan whined.

"No, girls, I'm the teacher and Lexi has to stay where she is," Madame Simpson said.

Then Madame Simpson let out a deep sigh, and turned her attention to one of her best-behaved students that day – Kaylee.

"Help, my feet are stuck!" Kaylee called, with both her feet stuck in the radiator.

"Oh, that's not fifth position! And where's your turnout?" Madame Simpson shrieked, getting down on the floor on her hands and knees, and freeing Kaylee's feet from the radiator.

"*Ahhh! I'm free!*" Kaylee screamed, toppling over Madame Simpson, and accidentally kicking her in the shin.

"OMG!" the class gasped.

Then Madame Simpson called:

"Girls! If I could have your attention! I know it's not easy, especially for *these* two feet, but you have to work on your turnout. I know you like to stand with your feet in a 'V,' but you need to start straightening them out for proper first position. See, Bianca's doing it right. Her heels are touching, and her feet make a straight line. Very nice work, Bianca!"

"Good job, Bee," Jessie nodded.

"You too, Jay. It's sort of tricky at first, but you'll get used to it. You're catching on really fast," Bianca grinned.

"Jessie, look at you. Very nice turnout. You're such a natural," Madame Simpson praised.

"Thanks! I got a real good teacher!" Jessie exclaimed.

"Thank you very much," Madame Simpson blushed.

"Oh yeah. You're good, too! But I was talkin' about Bee!"

"*Bee again?*" Megan gasped.

"Thanks, Jay!" Bianca cheered.

"*Jay?*" Jill went, and elbowed Courtney.

"Ooh, is there a bee? I collect them in a jar," Kaylee asked.

"You're so weird," Megan muttered.

"Megan, tuck in your tummy, and don't call Kaylee weird," Madame Simpson said.

"Oh, sorry," Megan replied, sucking in her stomach, and holding her breath.

"Now stop wheezing, Megan. Ballerinas don't wheeze. Stand up straight, and hold your head up high," Madame Simpson ordered.

"But my asthma," Megan shrugged.

"Turnout, Megan!" Madame Simpson called, clapping her hands, "Where's your turnout? You need to fix those sloppy feet!"

Then Megan suddenly ran off to the changing room.

"What happened to Megan?" Bianca asked.

And a couple minutes later, Megan returned to class, but she looked a little different.

Megan was now wearing a puffy white blouse, a black vest, and a short green skirt, with white knee socks, and a pair of wooden clogs on her feet. And she even had her hair up in short, red pigtails.

"O-M-G!" the whole class cried.

"I know. This is my outfit for clogging class. My mom's gonna be here any second. Sorry, Madame Simpson," Megan shrugged.

Then the class laughed.

"Hey, if I knew we were wearing costumes, I would've worn my French Can-Can outfit! It's a dance outfit, too! It's hot pink with black lace trim, and I'll bring in French music!" Bianca blurted.

"Oh Megan, look what you started. You're such a drama queen," their teacher sighed.

"Sorry. I guess my mom takes me to too many lessons, including drama," Megan joked.

"Well girls, I guess that's enough for today. Everyone gather around. It's time to talk about your toe shoes," Madame Simpson said.

Then she took a seat on her wooden stool, and the class sat on the floor around her.

Madame Simpson wore a knee-length blue ballet skirt, a powder blue leotard, and her favorite blue scarf tied around her head. Nobody could figure out how old she was, or even what color hair she had. She wore that same blue scarf every day.

"Well girls, I know I promised that you could try on the toe shoes today, but I just don't think you're ready yet," Madame Simpson said, fussing with her blue scarf.

"*What?*" Bianca gasped.

"What do you mean?" Megan asked.

"Why not?" the class complained.

"Because, *pointe* work is only for girls with strong ankles and feet. Some of you might be ready, but as a group . . . no. I just don't think you're ready yet," their teacher stated.

"But can't we just try on the toe shoes? I'm ready! *Please?*" Bianca begged.

"Sorry, Bianca, but this is a group class."

"*But I'm ready!*" Bianca repeated.

But Madame Simpson wouldn't change her mind.

"Girls, let's wait another week and see what happens. I don't want anyone to get hurt. But look on the bright side, we have all summer to try on the toe shoes. In the fall, it's only toe shoes. You'll be begging me to go back to ballet slippers. Trust me, this is for the best."

The girls whined and pouted, but deep down they knew she was right.

"Some of us are more ready than others," Jill huffed, giving Megan a nasty look.

"Yeah, and that little girl ith too tiny," Courtney lisped, pointing at Lexi.

Then Lexi frowned and hugged her knees.

"Silence! I'm warning you, Jill and Courtney. If you don't start behaving, I'll have to ask you to leave the class," their teacher said.

Then Jill and Courtney smacked their gum.

"And no more gum chewing!" Madame Simpson yelled.

"I *never* let my Megan chew gum! It's fattening!" called a loud voice from the back.

Everyone turned around, and saw Megan's mom interrupting class as usual.

"Not now, Mrs. Fields. I have just one more thing to say," their teacher said.

"Meggy, it's time for your voice lesson! Why are you wearing your clogging outfit? Your classes got switched, remember?" Mrs. Fields cried.

"Oh no," Megan sighed.

"Excuse us, Mrs. Fields. As I was saying . . ." their teacher interrupted.

"But Miss Simpson, I left the car running and we have to run! Megan, don't forget your mouth rinse. Last time you forgot it, and you sounded like a frog," Mrs. Fields said.

"*Mo-om!*" Megan cried, with her face turning a bright shade of red.

"Did you at least go to the bathroom?" her mom asked, "If not, we'll stop at Daddy's office."

"Oh, Mom," Megan groaned.

"Mrs. Fields, if you could wait just one more minute . . . oh, nevermind. Class dismissed," their teacher sighed.

5

the best house

Another week went by, and the girls still weren't allowed to try on Madame Simpson's old toe shoes. They were starting to get anxious, especially Bianca. She was busy counting up her pre-pointe hours, as she needed fifty hours by September first.

But when Bianca wasn't in ballet class, she was outside working on her tan at her fabulous McMansion. She was planning her big trip to Paris in the fall, and wondering if she should tell her new friends. But for now, she didn't want to spoil things by telling them she was leaving.

And if she told them she was moving to France, she thought they definitely wouldn't want to come to her pool party she was hoping to have.

Bianca loved to float around on her pool chair, with a soda in one hand, and her French dictionary in the other. She had to soak up as much French as she could before heading to France.

But sometimes, Bianca's carefree afternoons at the pool were interrupted by a very creepy and annoying next door neighbor.

"If I catch you looking at me with your binoculars one more time, I'm gonna have my mom call your mom!" she shouted into the bushes.

Hiding in the bushes, with his binoculars focused on Bianca, was none other than Bianca's neighbor, William Henry Covington the Fifth. He was the heir to his great-great-grandfather's toilet plunger fortune. His family invented the first ever rubber toilet plunger, and was super rich. His house was even bigger than Bianca's.

William, who went by Willy, was also eleven and going into sixth grade. He spent all his time watching *Star Trek* reruns and spying on Bianca through his giant binoculars.

"I'm warning you, Willy! You better stop spying on me, or I'm gonna tell my mother!" Bianca threatened.

Then Willy, with his slicked-back blonde hair, poked his head out from the bushes and yelled:

"Go ahead, but I'm still gonna marry you!"

Bianca got so grossed out, she considered getting up from her pool chair and dumping her soda all over him. But she decided to slurp it down instead.

40

"Why do I get stuck with this weird boy living next door?" she sighed.

Then her cell phone rang and she saw Jessie's last name on the screen.

"Hello, Bianca the Best here."

"Hey Bee, it's Jessie. Wassup?"

"Hi, Jessie! Are you doing something now?"

"Nah, all I got is my brother buggin' me to play ball with him, and I told him I'm a girl now."

"Ooh, you have a brother? Is he cute?"

"I dunno. He's my brother."

"Hmm. We'll talk about it later. Anyway, I was just gonna call you. You read my mind. I'm having a pool party today."

"You got a pool? I'll be over in five minutes."
Click.

"*Barrr-beee!*" Bianca called out to her mom.

"Yes, Bianca dear?" her mom replied, walking over to the pool, wearing a hot pink sundress and a pair of matching pink sandals.

"*Bonjour, Barbie!*" Bianca greeted.

"Oh my gosh! You sound so French!" her mom squealed.

"But Mom, it only means hello."

"Really? But you sounded so French. Can you teach me?" Barbie asked.

"*Oui!* You say it like 'we' and that means yes! But I have something important to ask you."

"Anything, Bianca. Do you wanna start packing your clothes for Paris?" Barbie asked.

"Well, not yet. I still have to read my dictionary. I think I'll pack next week," Bianca shrugged.

"Okay," Barbie nodded, tossing her long, fluffy blonde hair from side to side.

"Hmm, cute dress. That would look great on me in Paris! Can I borrow it?" Bianca asked.

"Sure, don't you borrow all my clothes? So what did you want to ask me? You said it was important."

"Oh, yeah. Can I have a pool party? I could really go for a pool party."

"Sure, when?"

"Today."

"Today? *Marrr-thaaa!*" Barbie called out to their maid, "Two dozen pigs in a blanket! And five gallons of ice cream! We're having a party!"

"Thanks, Mom! You're a great cook!"

"You're welcome, dear. It was nothing. So are Jill and Courtney coming? I haven't seen them in a little while."

"*Them?* They're history. I have new friends now. You'll meet them tonight. They're super nice and they all take ballet."

"Sure, Biancy," Barbie giggled.

"Ahem, I need to call my guests. Hint, hint," Bianca shooed her mom away.

"Sure, Biancy. I'll help Martha in the kitchen," her mom nodded.

Then Bianca called Megan to invite her to her pool party.

"*Hellooooowww?*"

"Megan? It's Bianca!"

"*Bee-on-caaaa?*"

"Megan? You sound weird. Are you okay?"

"I'm hanging upside down, so how do you think I'm doing?" Megan blurted.

"What?" Bianca asked.

"I'm hanging upside down from this ridiculous exercise machine! My mom bought it off some dumb infomercial. I think it's supposed to tone my abs or something."

"And you're talking upside down?" Bianca giggled.

"I can also eat a Twinkie upside down," Megan said proudly.

"Megan, what on earth is going on in your house?"

"My mom is driving me nuts. She's been on this buying binge, ever since she heard ballet's only half a day."

"*Buying binge?* That's usually a good thing."

"No, trust me, it's bad! My mom's been buying me exercise machines from TV infomercials every single day!"

"Oh no, Megan. How come?"

"She thinks I'm missing out on exercise because I'm not dancing in *pointe* shoes yet. She thought we were doing the New York City Ballet Workout. You know, the really hard one? But even *that* isn't as hard as this!"

"You poor thing," Bianca said.

"Yeah, I know. So what are you up to?"

Bianca paused, and knew Megan would be jealous if she could see her floating lazily around her pool.

"Oh, this and that," Bianca replied.

"This and that? Sounds better than what I'm doing. Hey, do you think you can come over and smuggle me some Twinkies?"

"I don't think I should, Megan. I'm too afraid of your mom."

"Too bad. So what are you calling about? Don't leave me hanging. Ha, ha! Get it?"

"That's a good one, Megan. So, I wanted to invite you to my pool party today. Jessie's coming too."

"Of course she is," Megan muttered.

"Huh?" Bianca went.

"Nothing. I'm there! I'll be over as soon as I can get off this dumb machine."

Click.

Bianca giggled, and paddled her chair over to the edge of the pool.

Then she called Lexi and Kaylee, and invited them too, and they happily accepted.

By the time she was off the phone with Kaylee, Jessie was already at her door ringing the bell.

"Hey Bee! Nice house," Jessie said.

"Hey Jay! Come in!" Bianca cheered, grabbing Jessie's arm.

"Oh my gosh, the guests are here? *So soon?*" Barbie called.

Then Barbie appeared from the kitchen, and sashayed over in her hot pink sundress.

"You got a twin?" Jessie asked.

"It's my mom," Bianca giggled.

"You're a mom?" Jessie shrugged. "But you look just like Bee. I don't believe it."

"Believe it, Jay. Here, let me give you a tour of the house," Bianca offered.

"Ooh, that sounds like fun! Mind if I come along?" Barbie asked.

"Mom, you live here!" Bianca laughed.

Then Barbie sashayed back to the kitchen to taste the party food.

"Shoot, I shoulda worn my hikin' boots. This place is huge!" Jessie called, with her mouth gaping wide open.

"This way, c'mon!" Bianca called, posing at the bottom of the stairs.

But Jessie just stood speechless in Bianca's grand marble foyer.

It was the biggest, fanciest house she ever saw.

She looked up at the high ceilings and crystal chandelier, and then her eyes moved down to the marble staircase and to the shiny marble floors.

"Nice! Should I take off my sneakers? I don't wanna mess up the floors," Jessie worried, adding, "Gees, did ya rob a museum? You got more paintings than at the school field trips!"

"OMG, I gotta brush my hair!" Bianca decided, grabbing Jessie's hand and pulling her up the tall marble staircase, all the way to her second floor master bedroom suite.

"Gosh, Bee, your house is really big! It's like a castle! In fact, I think it is! I mean, you could fit my entire apartment in ya livin' room!"

At the top of the marble staircase, and down the long hallway, was Bianca's master bedroom suite.

"Where's my brush? My hair's a total mess! I haven't brushed it for ten minutes!" Bianca cried, and grabbed her brush off her beautiful gold-plated vanity table.

"This is *your* bedroom? Ya mean only one person sleeps in here?" Jessie asked.

"Yeah, this is it," Bianca said, brushing her hair and fluffing it up.

Jessie's mouth gaped open again. She checked out the huge bedroom. She stared at the fireplace, the purple velvet sofa and chairs, the large pink canopy bed, and the biggest walk-in closet she had ever seen in her whole life.

"You're like a princess livin' here! When can I move in? Hey, tell your mom that my dad's single and really good lookin'! I wanna move in! Can I crash on your sofa?" Jessie asked.

Then Bianca put down her brush and giggled.

"Sure, you can come over all the time. Let's get ready for the party now," Bianca said.

"I'll be back for dinner tomorrow! What are we havin'?" Jessie cheered, and strutted into one of Bianca's walk-in closets.

"Oh, you have good taste! My shoe closet is the best room in the house, after my ballet closet of course!" Bianca called.

Jessie found herself surrounded by designer shoes in every color, arranged in rainbow order on fancy gold-plated shelves.

"This is just like Foot Locker!" she shouted.

"Keep going," Bianca said, and directed her to three other walk-in closets: her amazing clothes closet, her fabulous ballet closet, and her fancy designer handbags closet.

"You got four closets?" Jessie counted.

"Well, five, if you count my old toy closet. But that's in my old room."

"Your *old* room?"

"Uh-huh, after the divorce, Barbie and I switched rooms. So how's my hair?" Bianca asked.

"Cool! You look fab-u-lous!" Jessie replied, trying to talk like Bianca.

"Oh, your first fabulous! Love it!" Bianca squealed with delight.

Then Bianca skipped to her window, and began to watch for her party guests.

"Hey, what about my tour? I thought I was gettin' a tour?" Jessie reminded her.

"Okay, let's go!" Bianca exclaimed, grabbing Jessie's hand.

47

Then they ran upstairs to the third floor.

"So what's up here? Got another pool?" Jessie asked.

"No, silly! We got a roller ballroom! Do you rollerskate? Wanna skate now? I have skates in every size!" Bianca exclaimed, pulling Jessie into the huge roller ballroom.

"Whoa, dude! This place just keeps on gettin' bettah!" Jessie declared.

"C'mon, let's skate!" Bianca cheered, running into the ballroom, and turning on all the disco balls and awesome party music.

6

pool party

Two hours later, Megan finally arrived at Bianca's house. She didn't know the party had already started. Jessie beat her once again – and got to be the first one inside Bianca's house.

So when she showed up to the party, Megan was surprised to hear the party music blasting and see the rainbow disco lights flashing from the third floor windows.

"Whoa!" Megan cried, looking up at the party from inside her mom's parked car.

"I told you we were gonna be late," Mrs. Fields said, shaking her head.

Megan's mom was never actually late for anything, but she always thought she was.

"Oh my gosh! Bianca Best has a dance club in her house? *Mo-om!* Why'd you make me wear this? *I don't wanna wear my party dress, do I have to wear my party dress?*" Megan whined.

Megan was sitting in a way-too-tight, frilly pink party dress that she wore to a cousin's wedding two whole years ago.

"But Megan, you have to make a good impression. I complimented her on her leotard, so you have to do the rest. And why weren't you invited to Bianca's house before that new girl Jessie?" her mom pushed.

"Mom, can we go home so I can change? I look like a baby!" Megan insisted, turning red.

"Megan, this is a once in a lifetime opportunity to be invited to Bianca Best's house," Mrs. Fields declared.

"But Mom, this is *so embarrassing.* Nobody wears these dresses anymore."

"Oh Meggy, just be good. Ooh, I'm so excited that Bianca invited us to her house!"

"*Us?*"

"I've always wanted to see the inside of her house!" her mom cried.

"Mom, you're *not* invited," Megan stated.

"I wonder if Barbie's home?" her mom asked, not listening at all.

Megan sat sulking in her seat, when suddenly she noticed Jessie rollerskating by the window and holding hands with Bianca.

"Oh no, looks like Jessie's the best friend again! Sorry, gotta run!" Megan cried, undoing her seat belt, and making a mad dash out of the car.

"*Wait, Megan! Wait for me!*" her mom called.

"Sorry, Mom, see you later!"

Megan darted away from the wagon, and ran to Bianca's front door before her mom could follow her inside.

Mrs. Fields was annoyed at first, but she cheered up when she saw Megan running. At least Megan was burning some calories, she thought.

"Hi, Megan! Nice to see you!" Bianca greeted, panting from her run downstairs to the front door.

"Hi, Bianca! Let me in quick! My mom's about to follow me in here!"

Bianca let her in fast, closed the door, and looked through the peephole.

"You dressed up," Bianca said, checking out Megan's frilly pink party dress which was about to burst at the seams, as well as her frilly white socks and white patent leather Mary Janes.

"Yuck, my mom made me wear this. Do you have some jeans and a t-shirt I can change into?"

"Sure, upstairs in my room," Bianca said.

"Great, cuz I look like Shirley Temple right now," Megan joked, shaking her new tight curls.

"Or like the French girl, Madeline, with red hair. You know, the books that take place in Paris. Oops, I said Paris," Bianca blurted, and covered her mouth.

Then the girls raced up the marble stairs to the second floor, and ran straight to Bianca's room.

"Huh, Paris? Anyway, you have a cool house!" Megan called, walking into Bianca's room, and staring up at the huge crystal chandelier.

"Thanks," Bianca smiled, grabbing her brush off her gold vanity table.

"Nice table. Looks expensive!" Megan blurted.

"OMG, I guess it is! It's gold-plated. Anyway, my closet's over there. Go pick out an outfit, and don't get lost," Bianca giggled, and pointed to one of her large walk-in closets.

"Holy cow! Is this closet really all yours?" Megan gasped.

"Yeah, I know what you mean. It's just barely big enough," Bianca replied, spraying tons of hair spray all over her head.

"Um, I'll just take a look around – I could really use a map," Megan said, wandering into Bianca's enormous shoe closet.

"Okay, but I think I hear Jessie calling. Toodles!" Bianca called, and ran back upstairs to return to Jessie in the roller ballroom.

Then the doorbell rang, and Bianca turned around and raced back downstairs to the front door.

"Hi, Bianca! Can I come in?" Lexi asked, wearing a Care Bears swimsuit and yellow floaties on her arms.

"Hi, Lexi! Is someone ready to make a splash? Come on in, sweetie," Bianca cooed.

"Do you have a shallow end? I'm only allowed in the shallow end. It's the rules," Lexi asked.

"Of course I do, silly. Don't tell anyone, but that's only where I'm allowed, too," Bianca whispered, and played with Lexi's cute ponytail.

"He, he. You're nice! My mother doesn't play with my hair. Will you brush it?" Lexi asked.

"Oh Lexi, don't get me started. I can brush hair for days! You really pegged me! We're gonna be great BFF's!" Bianca smiled.

"We are? Yay, I like you!" Lexi giggled.

"The girls are all here except for Kaylee. Megan's in my closet, and Jessie's . . ."

"Hey Lil' Lexi! What's shakin'?" Jessie called, rollerskating down the stairs at the speed of light, and really scaring Bianca.

"Oh no, Jessie! What are you doing?" Bianca screamed.

"It's ah-ight. I made it down in one piece."

"Phew! Don't ever do that to me again, okay?" Bianca sighed.

Then the gang wanted to get the party started, and went to find Megan in Bianca's closets.

"Megan, there you are! You got lost in my closets, didn't you? It's common!" Bianca laughed, hunting down Megan in her handbag closet.

"Hi, Bianca! Gosh, all that designer stuff runs way too small. But this is great," Megan said, showing off her new Victoria's Secret dress.

"Megan, why are you wearing my nightshirt?" Bianca giggled.

Then Megan looked down at her pink cotton "dress" that had little stars and moons on it.

"*Your nightshirt?*" Megan shrieked, and shared a big laugh with Bianca.

After Bianca told Megan that it was totally normal to wear a nightshirt in public, the party finally got started and moved to the pool.

Bianca couldn't wait to show off her pink inflatable pool chair. She floated around for about five minutes, while Jessie claimed the hot tub, Megan plunked herself at the snack table, and Lexi stuck her toes in the shallow end.

Then Bianca paddled her chair over next to the hot tub, where Jessie was sitting, and asked her a really big question:

"So why haven't I known you my whole life?"

"I dunno? I'm new. Hey, cool underwater TV!"

"Yeah, huh? Works great at night. But seriously, where have you been?" Bianca asked.

"What? I'm tryin' to watch the Disney Channel. You got cable in your pool!" Jessie called.

"C'mon, Jessie, tell me your life story!"

Jessie didn't even hear that last question, but Megan, who was strategically located at the nearby snack table, heard everything. Jessie wasn't giving Bianca any attention, and Megan thought it was the perfect time to earn some points with Bianca.

Megan instantly swallowed the barely chewed hot dog in her mouth, shot up, and screamed:

"Ooh, ooh, Bianca, Bianca! Watch this!"

Then she bolted for the diving board. She sprinted off it, still wearing Bianca's nightshirt, and did a huge belly-flop into the deep end!

She made a thunderous noise and splashed half the water out of the pool.

"That's nice, Megan," Bianca said, and turned back to Jessie.

"That's it? Nice?" Megan muttered under her breath, and continued to do belly-flops for as long as Bianca was glued to Jessie.

That turned out to be a while.

"Jessie, where are you from?" Bianca asked.

"Queens, New York. The best place on earth! We got lotsa kids, lotsa things to do, and lotsa pizza!"

"Ooh, ooh, tell me more!"

"Ah-ight. We lived in Queens my whole life 'till now. Me and my dad and my two brothers. My mom lived there, too, but I don't remember."

"Huh?" Bianca asked, cocking her head.

"I, uh, don't talk about this with too many people. My mom went to heaven when I was three."

"Oh, I'm so sorry. I just thought your parents were divorced like mine," Bianca frowned.

"Lemme finish the story. We were okay in Queens, but the neighborhood got kinda rough, even for me. So my dad said we're movin' to the country for fresh air and good schools," Jessie said.

"Oh, we have great schools. I'll tell you more later," Bianca said, and then gave a dog a bone by complimenting Megan on her fifty belly-flops.

"Very nice, Megan. Now get the hose, and put some water back in the pool."

"OMG! *Very* nice? Yes! I went from *nothing* nice to *very* nice! Yes!" Megan jumped for joy, and then went back to the snack table to snag some juicy hot dogs from hot off the grill.

"Hey look, somebody's coming!" Lexi called.

The girls all turned around, and saw someone climb up the chain link fence from Willy's backyard, and get stuck at the top. The person teetered there for a few seconds, and then fell straight down into the bushes on Bianca's side.

"Who's there?" Bianca called, "If that's you, Willy, I'm getting my water gun!"

"It's me, Kaylee," the voice said.

"*Kaylee?*" everyone gasped.

"Where ya been?" Jessie asked.

"I went to the wrong house," Kaylee shrugged.

"You mean you were next door at Willy's house the whole time? OMG!" Bianca shrieked.

"Yeah, he's really cool! He's got a toilet plunger museum in his house, and he gave me a tour of it! *It was so neat!* Way better than Disney World!"

Then everyone laughed, and splashed water at Kaylee – whatever water was left after Megan's belly-flop marathon.

7

on our toes

The next week in class, the girls were definitely a tight group, and everyone could see it.

"I'm such a good teacher! You're all friends because of my assignment to go to the mall," Madame Simpson boasted, and then asked, "Wait, aren't you missing two friends?"

Then the girls exchanged looks, as if to say:

"What? She thinks we're friends with Jill and Courtney?"

Then, about fifteen minutes after class started, Jill and Courtney finally strolled in.

"We're here. You can start class now," Jill declared, smacking her gum and carrying her flashy silver dance bag.

"Hey, we didn't mith much," Courtney lisped, carrying an empty bottle of Evian, and wearing big gold hoop earrings.

"Jill and Courtney, may I see you for a moment?" Madame Simpson asked, taking Jill and Courtney to the side.

She scolded them for being late to class. She said ballerinas can't be late for performances, can't chew gum on stage, or in class – and worst of all, they can't wear big, heavy hoop earrings, even if they have your name in script across the middle.

Jill and Courtney had the worst attitudes now. They couldn't stand Bianca, and they especially couldn't stand Bianca's new friends.

So Megan was an easy target for them.

It didn't take long into warm-ups for them to start teasing her.

"Megan's a cow," Jill hissed.

"*Moooo,*" Courtney joined in.

"Megan the moo-cow," Jill laughed.

"Megan the moo-cow," Courtney repeated.

"Let's call her Moo-gan!" Jill decided.

"Jill, you're funny. Hey Moo-gan!" Courtney called.

"Pipe down you dogs!" Jessie defended Megan.

"Look who's calling us dogs. Jessie the dog!" Jill called.

"*Bark, bark,*" Courtney went.

"Who let the dogs out?" Jill laughed.

"*Woof, woof,*" Courtney barked.

"You're such babies!" Bianca called.

"Did you hear something?" Jill asked Courtney, giving Bianca the silent treatment.

"No, nobody," Courtney replied.

"Oh, it's Miss Piggy!" Jill laughed, pointing at Bianca.

"*Oink, oink,*" Courtney went.

"*Oink, oink,*" Jill repeated.

"Um, stop it, bad girls," Lexi whispered.

"Did you hear something, Courtney? I think the little mouse spoke," Jill asked.

"*Thqueak, thqueak,*" Courtney lisped.

"Stop it!" Lexi repeated, now a little louder.

"Stop it!" Jill copied her in a very high-pitched voice.

"Thtop it!" Courtney echoed.

"Farmer Bianca, your animals got loose from their pens!" Jill yelled.

But Madame Simpson heard Jill's last remark.

"Jill, that was awfully mean – even for you. Go stand in the corner," she ordered.

But Madame Simpson's punishment only made Jill even meaner.

When the time came to practice running leaps, their teacher lined them up on one side of the room. She told the girls to perform a running leap one at a time, and across the room. But just Megan's luck, the landing spot was Jill's corner.

"*Moooooo!*" Jill moaned at Megan, every time it was Megan's turn to take a running leap.

Megan tried to ignore Jill, but she found it hard when Jill started milking invisible udders in the air every time Megan did a leap.

Courtney lost it every time. When it was her turn, she did terrible little leaps, giggling and holding her tummy the whole way.

Later into class, Jill came up with another dumb put-down for Megan.

"You're so fat! You look like a dancing hippo!" Jill declared.

"No, I don't!" Megan yelled back.

"Yeth, you do!" Courtney fired, from right behind Megan in line.

When Megan took her next running leap, which again landed her in front of Jill's corner, Jill meanly informed her:

"Megan, you're making the whole place shake. You're gonna break the floors."

"No, I'm not!"

"Yeah, you are! You're so fat, you're gonna break the whole building down!"

"No, I'm not!"

"Oh yes, you are! And then you know what? Bianca's not gonna like you anymore. Not after you break her precious studio. She's gonna *hate* you. Just like I do."

At that moment, Megan turned around so Jill wouldn't see her crying. Then she ran right into the changing room, and grabbed her dance bag on the way out.

"Megan, where are you going? Is your mother here already?" Madame Simpson called.

But Megan had already disappeared down the hall.

Jill laughed meanly to herself, and proudly smacked her gum in victory.

"Wait, Megan!" Bianca called, running out of the studio.

Megan ran downstairs, and stopped on the second floor to hide in an empty room. It had a sign on the door that read: "Bridal Suite."

She grabbed an old wedding veil that was tacked on the wall for decoration, and blew her nose with it. Then she sneezed from all the dust.

Still sneezing, Megan was shocked when Bianca ran in to take care of some personal business.

Not knowing Megan was right there, Bianca yanked off her fake hair bun. She thought to herself how lucky she was that she could use running after Megan as a break to fix her loose hair bun in the privacy of her secret Bridal Suite.

But just as Bianca was tightening the elastic around her small natural bun, and placing the large and beautiful fake hair bun over it, Megan burst out laughing.

"Holy cow! It's a wig!" Megan cried.

"Hold on . . . done! OMG, did you just see me, um, play with my beautiful bun?" Bianca asked, worried that someone found out her secret.

61

"No, I saw you take your hair off!" Megan exclaimed, still laughing.

"Oh well, now you know Bianca Best wears hair extensions. Don't tell anyone?" Bianca asked, getting nervous.

"Don't worry, I won't. Hey, why do you wear those fake buns? Don't most people just use their own hair?" Megan giggled.

"That's only because most people don't have their own custom-made, ballet hair buns from Paris! I have ten fake buns in assorted platinum blonde colors, just in case my hair stylist dyes my hair wrong. Oh shoot, should I have said that?" Bianca blurted, covering her mouth.

"It won't leave this room. Hey, can I try on one of your fake buns? With my short hair, I can't ever make a bun."

"Oh sure, you can try on my spare, and while you're at it, why don't you fix your makeup?"

"Uh, I don't have any," Megan admitted.

"But don't you have some lip gloss in your dance bag?" Bianca asked.

"Uh, no."

"Oh, you left it at home?"

"Uh, no."

"Megan, if it isn't in your bag, and it isn't at home, then . . . you don't have any makeup?"

"Nope."

"Well, it's a good thing you got me. I got lots of gloss in my bag," Bianca said, searching her bag.

"Oh my gosh, Bianca. Thanks a lot! You're so awesome and you're so much fun!" Megan cried.

"*I am?* More please," Bianca giggled.

"You're so easy to talk to, and it's like I can tell you anything – just like a real best friend!"

"Okay! Let's be best friends!" Bianca decided.

"*Reeeeally?* Awesome!" Megan cheered, going for a big hug.

But then Megan accidentally knocked Bianca's tote bag off her shoulder, and all of Bianca's makeup and brushes spilled onto the floor.

And so did something else.

Right there on the floor, in plain view, was Bianca's acceptance letter to the Paris Pirouette program!

"Oh sorry, best friend! Lemme pick that up for you!" Megan offered, dropping to the floor.

"OMG! No, um, let me. I'll get it all. You, um, look the other way!" Bianca panicked, also dropping to the floor.

"Huh? Oh, what's that?" Megan asked, pointing to the letter, and grabbing it before Bianca could get it away from her.

"Oh nothing, best friend. Just gimme," Bianca barked, reaching for the letter in Megan's hands.

"Ooh, I know what this is! Holy snap! This is an acceptance letter to that fancy ballet school in Paris! I know about it! What are you doing with one of these?" Megan demanded, looking right at Bianca.

But it took a second for Bianca to reply.

"I, um, sorta sent away for information about the school, you know, for the future," Bianca tried.

"No you didn't! My mom's been sending them my application for years. And I *never* got in. Not once. You gotta have really good technique to get in, and wait – you do! You got in! You got into the Paris Pirouette program!" Megan realized.

"Um . . ." Bianca stalled.

"OMG! You're going this fall! That's next month! You're going in September, aren't you? That's when it starts! But wait, it just hit me. *You're going away?*" Megan gasped.

"Well . . ." Bianca stalled some more.

"OMG! And you weren't gonna tell me, were you?" Megan demanded.

Then Bianca paused, scratched her nose, and came up with something to say.

"Oh Megan, you totally got the wrong idea! Like I said, I just wanted information. I didn't say I was going. Besides, you need fifty hours of pre-pointe to go there, and I have about two. Well, more than that, but you know what I mean. We haven't even tried on toe shoes yet! How am I supposed to be a ballerina in Paris?"

And luckily, Megan fell for it.

"Yeah, you're right! We haven't even tried on toe shoes yet! You can't be a ballerina in Paris! You don't have fifty hours of pre-pointe! Oh phew, I'm so glad you're not going!" Megan blurted, wiping the sweat off her forehead.

Toe·tally Fabulous

"See? I told you the letter was nothing. Just do me a big favor, okay? Don't tell anyone? Best friends don't spill secrets," Bianca hoped.

"*Best friends?* I'll never tell! Never, ever, ever!" Megan swore, hopping up and down.

"Good, so let's forget about it and do your lip gloss now," Bianca smiled.

"Thanks, Bianca! You're the best!"

"That *is* my name. He, he."

"Um, Bianca, now that we're best friends, can I call you Bee?" Megan asked.

"Sure you can!"

"Um, Bee, now that we're best friends, can I have a big makeover like Jessie?"

"Ooh, sounds like fun! I have just the right colors to bring out your emerald green eyes and pretty auburn hair. You're a perfect Autumn. But when Bianca Best does a makeover, it takes all day! So let's see if we can do a quickie on your eyes, cheeks, lips, and hair – in the next five minutes! They'll start to miss me in class you know. I *am* the Junior Instructor."

They just made it back to class with five minutes left. Megan returned gleaming, knowing she was Bianca's best friend.

And she also knew two big secrets.

Megan smacked her lip gloss-covered lips at Jill, tossed her brushed and fluffed red hair, and strutted into the room with a really big smile.

65

Jill and Courtney rolled their eyes, and decided to ignore Megan. They focused their attention instead on what stores to go to at the mall after class. Then they thought about which stores to go to right now, and bolted out the door.

The day had suddenly turned around for Megan, and to the delight of the girls, Madame Simpson surprised the class by allowing them to try on her toe shoes for the very first time.

Together, the five friends stepped into the beautiful toe shoes, and waited for their teacher to tie their ribbons, and give them the nod to stand up.

Once in the shoes, they rocked back and forth on their toes, grabbed each other's hands for support, and cheered, "*Yay! We're doing it!*"

Then Megan lost her balance, and fell over onto Kaylee.

"Well, I *did* it!" Megan laughed at herself.

"Did what?" Kaylee asked, poking her big toe through a brand new hole she had just made in one of Madame Simpson's prized toe shoes.

"*Oh, Kaylee!*" they all sang.

"What? My toe has to go somewhere."

Then the girls laughed, and tried it all over again.

8

the turning point

After that amazing class, Bianca hugged her ballet friends goodbye and hopped into her mom's SUV parked in front of the Community Center.

"Hi, Mom! I did it, I did it! I went up on toe! I can't believe it! It was *toe*-tally fabulous!" Bianca exclaimed, buckling her seatbelt.

"Oh Biancy, you did? I'm so proud of you! Was it hard? How do your little toesies feel?" her mom asked, starting the engine.

"They're great. And it wasn't hard at all. But I could sure go for a touch-up on my pedicure. I think I broke a toenail. But I loved it anyway!"

"Oh no! You broke a toenail? Which one? Not your little baby toe?" her mom feared.

67

"No, my big toe. On my right foot. But my baby toes are just fine. Anyway, I'm totally not complaining. I really, really, really loved *pointe!*" Bianca insisted.

"I'm glad, Biancy. You've worked a long time to get up to *pointe.* We've been coming to the Community Center since you were five. Remember when you were five, Biancy? We used to go for ice cream after ballet."

"You mean we're not now?" Bianca gasped.

"Oh Biancy, I already bought you ice cream! It was supposed to be a surprise, but you've got tons of Ben and Jerry's waiting for you in the freezer," Barbie giggled, turning onto Main Street.

"Yay!" Bianca squealed with delight.

"You know, Biancy, it's very sweet of you to have an ice cream party with me after class. But I won't feel bad if you want to call up Jill and Courtney and invite them over."

Then the SUV went silent.

"O-M-G! Are you kidding me? Mom, I told you Jill and Courtney are *not* my friends anymore," Bianca declared.

"You mean you're still having a little tiff?" Barbie asked innocently.

"*A little tiff?* Oh Barbie, it's so much more than that. You wouldn't believe the way Jill and Courtney treated Megan today in ballet. They called her a cow and a dancing hippo, and they called Jessie a dog, Lexi a mouse, and me a farmer!"

"Huh? But that doesn't sound like Jill and Courtney," Barbie shrugged.

"What? Yes, it does. They're like the meanest girls now. Barbie, what's up? You still like Jill and Courtney?" Bianca asked.

"No, Biancy. I'm just trying to follow it all."

"Well, basically Jill and Courtney have changed. They're not who they used to be. And they don't care about ballet anymore. They weren't even there when we tried on the toe shoes!"

"Really, Biancy? That's too bad. They were such good friends. You were so close," Barbie said, frowning.

"I know, but now I have really fabulous friends! Megan, Jessie, Lexi, and Kaylee! They're like my dream friends. I don't know how I'm ever gonna move to Paris in September. Megan saw my letter, but I told her I wasn't going. I might not . . ."

"*Really?* You might not go to Paris, to stay with your new friends? Then maybe you want to invite them for a sleepover?" Barbie asked excitedly.

"OMG, I'd love to have a sleepover! But I haven't decided about Paris yet. I still might go."

Then they turned onto their street, Covington Farms Court. It was named for Willy's family, the Covingtons. Bianca and Willy had the only two houses on the street. It used to be all farmland owned by the Covingtons. It was a picture perfect, tree-lined street with Bianca's white, stonefront house and Willy's brick mansion right next door.

69

But then the picture perfect scene suddenly changed when Bianca caught a glimpse of her two former friends sitting on her front porch.

"What took you so long?" Jill demanded.

"Yeah, what took you tho long?" Courtney asked.

Then they got up from Bianca's front steps and waited to be let into the house.

"O-M-G! What are the two of you doing here?" Bianca wailed, running up to her front door.

"My mom dropped us off," Jill replied.

"But I thought you were going to the mall or something?" Bianca asked.

"No, guess not," Jill shrugged.

"Nope," Courtney added.

"So what are you doing at my house?" Bianca demanded.

"Well, I'll just go inside while you girls work things out," Barbie said, tip-toeing past them and into the house.

"*Work things out?* As if," Bianca huffed.

Then Jill and Courtney exchanged looks.

"Bianca, what's up with you? Why do you act like you hate us?" Jill asked.

"What?" Bianca went.

"Don't deny it. You totally ditched us for Megan and those new girls," Jill accused her.

"No, I didn't. It was your choice to fake sick and ditch our mall walk!" Bianca argued.

"Whatever. I guess I can forget it. *Still friends?*" Jill asked, smiling at Bianca.

"Leth go in now?" Courtney suggested.

"No way! You can't go in, and we're *not* friends," Bianca insisted, blocking her front door.

"What's the deal?" Jill snapped.

"Yeah, do you hate uth?" Courtney asked.

Bianca thought about it for a few seconds, and then answered with:

"I don't really hate you, but I hate the way you treated Megan and my friends. I couldn't believe the way you mooed at Megan and made her cry in front of everyone. And she's *not* fat! That was so mean! Gosh, have you two changed."

"Is that what's wrong? Come on, Bianca. It was funny," Jill said, chuckling.

"Tho funny!" Courtney agreed.

"No it wasn't! You made Megan cry!" Bianca fought.

"So? It's not my fault she's so sensitive," Jill replied.

"Well you're not sensitive at all," Bianca said, taking a seat on her front step.

Then Jill and Courtney stared at each other, shrugged, and then sat down next to Bianca.

"Well you know, Bianca, we're mad at you too. You got us in trouble today. Madame Simpson hates us now," Jill said, sighing.

"What? Are you trying to make me feel sorry for you? Cuz it's not working," Bianca said.

"OMG, I didn't know it was such a big deal. It was just ballet class. Why are you getting so serious about it and taking *pointe?*" Jill blurted.

"Jill, you know I love ballet! I'm so excited to take *pointe,* and I thought we were gonna take it together," Bianca explained.

"We're only in it cuz you're in it. Me and Court wanna take hip-hop," Jill admitted.

"Yeah. Come with uth to hip-hop?" Courtney asked.

"*Hip-hop?* But I'm gonna be a professional ballerina! Why would I ever drop *pointe?*" Bianca gasped.

"I dunno. You really wanna stay in ballet with those losers? Cuz if you do, then you're not cool enough to hang out with us," Jill snapped.

"*Really?*" Courtney gasped.

Then Bianca got up, dusted off the seat of her leotard, and said:

"Well, I guess that's it then. I didn't know it was gonna end like this, but I don't wanna be friends with mean girls. I'd show you to the door, but you're already outside."

"Well, we don't need you!" Jill fired.

"Yeth we do," Courtney blurted.

"Court, let's go. This place is lame," Jill said, walking down the driveway.

Then Bianca hurried inside to her big window to watch Jill and Courtney walk down the street. And then she knew what she had to do.

9

the sleepover

Tonight Bianca was hosting her first sleepover with her new ballet friends! She couldn't wait to celebrate their first time wearing toe shoes.

But she also had a *very* special surprise planned for them that was sure to knock their socks off.

"Yay, you're back! Did you invite everybody?" Bianca asked, greeting her maid, Martha, as she came through the front door.

"Yes, Miss Bianca, it's all set," Martha said, wearing a 1950's style costume. She wore a gray poodle skirt, a fuzzy pink sweater, and a pair of black and white saddle shoes.

"Did you remember to sing *Grease* songs when you gave out the invitations?" Bianca asked.

"Oh yes, it was so much fun! I gave out your invitations and sang 'Grease is the Word.' And I did the Hand Jive too, just as you asked. The girls were so surprised!" Martha smiled.

"Awesome! But did you do the *bop-bop-bop* before the *ding-ding-ding?* That's important you know," Bianca asked.

"Oh, I wouldn't dream of *ding-ding-dinging* before *bop-bop-bopping!*"

"Good, because if the girls say that you dinged before you bopped, then we did it all wrong!"

"Oh Miss Bianca, can I change now? These saddle shoes are two sizes too small."

"Sorry, but not until after you've greeted all the guests, and do your big opening number. You do know all the *lama-lamas* and *rama-ramas,* right?"

"I think so."

"Thank you, Martha! You're awesome! OMG, they're gonna be here any minute!"

"I better go fix my ponytail!" Martha called, and quickly ran to a mirror.

Just ten minutes later, the doorbell rang.

"Ooh, ooh! My first guest! Wonder who it is? Martha, you're on!" Bianca cheered, and watched Martha race to the front door.

"*You're the one that I want! Ooh, ooh, ooh, honey! The one that I want!*" Martha sang, opening the door and doing the Hand Jive at the same time, just like in the movie *Grease.*

74

"Quick, close the door!" Megan called, running in wearing her pink party dress again.

"No, Megan, you did it wrong! You didn't let Martha sing to you! Go back outside and do it again!" Bianca ordered.

"Really? But my mom will wanna come in and do the Twist!" Megan feared, tugging her suitcase.

Ding-dong!

"Oh no, see?" Megan insisted.

"*Rama-rama,* welcome to Bianca's *Grease* sleepover party! Ballet is the word!" Martha sang, opening the door again.

"Hey wassup? We're eatin' greasy food? That's my favorite!" Jessie cheered, and strutted in.

"No, Jessie. Not *greasy* food. *Grease* the movie!" Bianca giggled.

"Oh snap! You mean we're not having greasy food?" Megan asked.

"OMG, of course we are! It *is* a party!" Bianca exclaimed.

"Hey, it's the singin' lady again. I love that disco outfit," Jessie declared, getting it all wrong.

"Um, hi," someone suddenly squeaked.

"*Lexi?* Hi there! Where did you come from?" Bianca asked.

"Um, I was standing behind Jessie," Lexi said.

"So come in and join the party!" Bianca called, taking Lexi's violin and putting it to the side.

"So, we all here? Let's get the pah-ty started!" Jessie called, dropping her backpack on the floor.

"*Potty started?* Why? Do you have to start it? Will I not know how to work it here?" Lexi asked.

"OMG! I think Jessie means *par-tay!* Right over here, girls!" Bianca called, leading the group into the living room.

The room was decked out in *Grease* posters, balloons, and even life-size cut-outs of the stars of the movie, Sandy and Danny!

Bianca was super lucky to get the decorations from the party store, as eighth-grader Sandy Shapiro wanted them for her *Grease* bat mitzvah.

"What are we watchin' again?" Jessie asked, kicking back on the sofa with her feet up on the coffee table, right next to the dainty plate of gourmet chocolates.

"*Grease,* Jessie! And don't get your feet in the chocolate truffles," Bianca sighed.

"I've seen this movie like a million times," Megan complained.

"Oh really, is that so?" Bianca snapped, getting annoyed.

"And I can't wait to see it again!" Megan cheered, taking the hint.

"Is this movie rated G? I'm only allowed to watch G movies," Lexi informed them.

"Then *Bambi* it is," Megan said, rolling her eyes.

"Oh, and my bedtime's eight," Lexi added, "But if I get tired early, can someone put me to bed?"

"This kid's gonna be a lotta fun," Jessie joked.

"A regular party animal!" Megan laughed.

"Shh, don't make fun of her," Bianca hushed, and added, "Listen, Lexi, you're gonna have a good time watching a PG movie and you're gonna stay up all night, and you're gonna love it!"

Then Bianca hit the "play" button on her remote and started the movie.

Jessie and Megan exchanged looks and wondered when they would get to eat the party food.

But they didn't have to wait too long.

There was one more girl on the guest list, and she was about to really get things cooking!

"Hi guys," Kaylee said, strolling into the living room, and appearing out of nowhere.

"*Kaylee?*" everyone went.

"Where did you come from?" Bianca asked, pausing the movie.

"My house," Kaylee replied, and then headed to the front door.

"See ya!" Megan called after her.

"Thanks for comin'!" Jessie added, snickering with Megan.

"Wait, Kaylee! *You're leaving?* But I didn't give you your goody bag!" Bianca called after her, running to the door.

But to Bianca's surprise, she bumped into a parade of a dozen uniformed waiters!

Rushing through the door, they marched into the living room and began to set up five buffet tables and lots of platters of food.

"Wait, who are you? I ordered pizza and Chinese food, and I don't see my egg rolls?" Bianca asked, checking out the dishes.

"Guys, these are my brothers, sisters, and cousins. We brought over some snacks for the party from our diner. So enjoy!" Kaylee explained, digging into a platter of hot Greek gyros.

"Now you're talking! Great party, Bee! I'm starving! Hey Jessie, grab me a plate?" Megan called, licking her chops and smelling all the hot food.

"No problem, M-dawg!" Jessie called back, tossing Megan a paper plate through the air.

"*M-dawg?* Hey, I'm the one who gives out the nicknames. It's *my* sleepover party, and it's *my* house. *Wah!* And where are my egg rolls?" Bianca pouted.

"Mmm! Chocolate pudding!" Lexi cheered, eating right out of a huge container of pudding.

"Watch the liquids, kid. We're watchin' a movie," Jessie warned, watching Lexi suck up the sugary chocolate pudding with a straw.

"Whoa! Great idea, Lexi! I'm gonna try that!" Megan cheered, grabbing two straws and sucking up tons of mashed potatoes and gravy – right through the straws.

"Have a hot gyro! Gyros are the best!" Kaylee sang, serving a gyro to Megan.

"Hey, save some room for the gourmet pizzas I ordered!" Bianca whined.

"But what about the egg rolls?" Megan asked, with gravy dripping down her face and all over her frilly pink party dress.

Just then, Martha ran in to serenade the "guests" who had just arrived.

"Grease is the word!" she sang to Kaylee's family who thought she was singing about the country Greece.

"No, Martha. I told you, only sing to the guests, not the delivery men," Bianca giggled.

"But where are the egg rolls?" Martha asked, loading up her poodle skirt with some fries and onion rings.

"OMG, who knows? Let's just dig in!" Bianca decided, grabbing a plate.

And for the next two hours, the girls pigged out, watched *Grease,* and cheered on Martha as she acted out every song and dance in the movie!

10

new ballet shoes

When they finished the movie, Bianca moved everyone upstairs for Part Two of the party.

"I have a surprise!" Bianca called, and plunked down on her bed with her friends.

"Ooh, ooh! You got us a surprise? Me first, me first!" Megan blurted.

"Cool! More food?" Jessie asked.

"Did you get something for Harry? I brought him, see?" Kaylee asked, pulling Harry out of her pocket, and placing him on Bianca's satin pillow.

"*Ahhhh!*" Bianca shrieked.

"*Hiccup,*" Lexi interrupted.

"Kaylee, remove that rodent from my pillow at once!" Bianca ordered.

80

"Okay," Kaylee said, and lifted Harry off Bianca's pillow, and put him back in her pocket.

"As I was about to say, Megan's absolutely right. I do have presents for you! But they're not just any presents! They're *membership* presents!" Bianca announced.

"Membership? To what, the Y?" Jessie asked.

"Oh no, not the gym?" Megan feared.

"Does this mean I can use your pool for free?" Jessie asked.

"*Hiccup,*" Lexi chimed in.

"Quiet! If you keep talking, I won't be able to give you your awesome Ballet Ladies shoes!" Bianca blurted.

"*What?*" they all asked.

"You heard me. Jessie, Megan, Lexi, and Kaylee, I totally invite you to join my new fabulous club, the Ballet Ladies!" Bianca cheered.

"O-M-G!" they cried.

"And as the leader of the Ballet Ladies, it is my pleasure to present your official Ballet Ladies club shoes! Yay!"

Then Bianca handed each girl a big, black shopping bag with the name "Chanel" across it.

"No way! Chanel ballet flats? They match your bag! Thanks *sooo* much!" Megan shrieked, tearing open her gift bag and putting on the shoes.

Then Megan started dancing crazy and singing:

"*Boom-boom, snap-snap! Boom-boom, snap! Boom-boom, snap-snap! Boom-boom, snap!*"

Then everyone laughed at Megan's new song, and Bianca even joined in.

"Cool, we're in a club!" Jessie exclaimed.

"*Hiccup!* Thank you," Lexi said, with chocolate pudding all over her face.

"Look, a new bed for Harry!" Kaylee cheered, admiring the shoe box and tossing the expensive shoes over her shoulder.

"*Oh, Kaylee!*" they all sang.

The girls slipped on their new ballet flats, and admired the big CC logo on their toes and the pretty quilted leather. But most of all, they loved that Bianca Best chose them to be her new best friends.

"Awesome!" Jessie exclaimed, checking out her black ballet flats.

"Hey, they fit!" Megan cheered, hopping up and down in her white ballet flats.

"Great! Because my mom ordered them all the way from Paris," Bianca blurted, and then paused.

"*Paris?* Um, never heard of it," Megan joked.

"Ooh, I love my silver shoes!" Lexi squealed, wearing her small silver flats.

"Hey, do these shoes come in orange? Mind if I paint them orange?" Kaylee asked, holding up her tan shoes.

"Oh, Kaylee! Paint them orange and you're dead meat!" Bianca snapped, wearing her own new pair of pink ballet flats.

Then the girls took a couple minutes to just take it all in and enjoy the moment.

"Hey guys, you're supposed to say thanks when ya get free stuff," Jessie said, and added, "Thanks, Bee! You're the best!"

"Ballet Ladies, it's my pleasure. If we're gonna be best friends forever, then we just gotta have the cutest club shoes! You know, we're gonna be the most *fabulous* girls in school!" Bianca squealed with delight.

"We're so fabulous! We're *toe*-tally fabulous!" Megan announced.

"OMG! Toe-tally! That's what I say, too! You're awesome, Megan!" Bianca exclaimed.

"I know," Megan replied, talking like Bianca.

"Ya mean our toes are fabulous?" Jessie asked, shrugging.

Then Bianca and Megan shared a BFF moment and laughed together.

"Harry's toes are fabulous, too!" Kaylee added.

"*Oh, Kaylee!*" everyone sang.

"O-M-G! I just had one of my Best Ideas! From now on, Kaylee is Kay! It's super cool!" Bianca suddenly decided.

"Fine with me. So what's Harry's new name?" Kaylee asked.

"I don't do rodent names," Bianca replied.

"Hey! How come the klutz gets a nickname and I don't?" Megan complained.

"Megan, from now on, Kay is no longer called the klutz. She's one of us, and therefore she's Kay. Just Kay. *Okay?*" Bianca insisted.

"Huh? You called me?" Kaylee asked, looking around.

"OMG!" everyone cried.

Then there was a knock at the door.

"Who is it?" Bianca asked.

"It's me, Barbie!"

"Come on in," Bianca said.

"Hi girls! Oh my gosh, you look so cute in your matching ballet flats. I'm ready for our sleepover," Barbie said, carrying her sleeping bag.

Then everyone giggled.

"Mom, you know it's just for the Ballet Ladies. But thanks for the shoes," Bianca giggled.

"Oh gumdrops. Okay, have a good sleepover. But can I talk to you in the hall?" Barbie asked.

"What's up, Mom? But aren't you gonna miss *The Brady Bunch?*" Bianca asked, going to the hall.

"Um, I got another letter from the Paris Pirouette program, and um, you can't go," Barbie blurted.

"*What?*" Bianca gasped.

"I'm sorry, Bianca bear. It says here you need five hundred hours of pre-pointe class. Not fifty. The first letter had a typo. They forgot a zero."

"OMG! I can't believe it! You know what this means? My troubles are over – now I don't have to choose between Paris and my BFF's! I get to stay!"

"Yippee! You're staying here!" Barbie cheered, and skipped away singing *The Brady Bunch* theme song, "*Here's the story of a lovely lady who was bringing up three very lovely girls.*"

Toe-tally Fabulous

"*All of them had hair of gold like their mother, the youngest one in curls!*" Megan chimed in, after listening at the door.

Then all the girls laughed and sang along.

"OMG! Do you just wanna go downstairs and watch *The Brady Bunch* with my mom? Or do you wanna hang out with me and be Ballet Ladies?" Bianca asked, winking at Megan.

"I'll stay here. I don't know what song they're singin' anyway," Jessie said.

"Good answer, Jay," Bianca nodded.

"Wait, wait! Me too, me too! I don't know what I was just singing!" Megan claimed.

"I do! It's the best show on TV! Can I really go downstairs with your mom?" Kaylee asked.

"Kay dear, look down at your new fancy shoes, and tell me who gave you them and whose club you just joined? Hmm?" Bianca snapped.

"Hey Kay, I think you should stay right here. Bee's got some good stuff planned. Tell her, Bee!" Jessie nudged.

"Oh, um, that's right! I have so much planned. Let's see, we already ate. So who wants to have a blast rollerskating?" Bianca cheered.

"Hey, that sounds like exercise. Next idea!" Megan called.

"Okay then . . . how about spa time? Yay! Mud masks are the funnest!" Bianca cheered again.

"Huh? Put mud on my face? No way. Next!" Jessie called.

85

"Okay . . . how about makeovers? I have the *best* makeup!" Bianca boasted.

"I'm not allowed. It's the rules," Lexi replied.

"OMG! What a tough crowd," Bianca sighed, and then asked, "Ooh, I know! How about I curl everyone's hair?"

"No thanks. I already have curly hair. And so does Harry," Kaylee replied.

"OMG! I give up! I'm the funnest person, and you guys keep saying no to all my Best Ideas!" Bianca cried, rolling her eyes and falling back on her bed.

"Hey Bee, I know! Since we got the upstairs to ourselves, wanna call some boys?" Jessie asked, reaching for the phone.

"Hey, how did you get Harry's cell phone number?" Kaylee asked.

"*Oh, Kaylee!*" they all sang.

"Wait, we called her Kaylee!" Bianca giggled, adding, "But I'll allow it this once."

"Then it's okay, everyone," Megan said, letting everyone know.

"Thanks, Megan," Bianca laughed.

"Back to boys. So who do we call first? Ya know the number of that Willy kid?" Jessie asked.

"Oh no, Jessie! Creepy Willy? You've gotta be kidding. No way! He'll think I *like* him!" Bianca shrieked.

"Well, I kinda think you do!" Jessie teased, "You're always talkin' about him."

"*Eww!* You didn't just say that! Change the topic!" Bianca cried, blushing.

"I know who we can call!" Megan exclaimed.

"Who?" everyone asked.

"Mario!" Megan cheered.

"*Mario?* Who's that? Is he in our grade?" Bianca asked.

"*Mario's Pizza! Ha ha ha ha ha!*" Megan roared, tilting her head back in a fit of laughter.

"Oh Megan! You got me real good!" Bianca laughed.

"I made you laugh!" Megan called.

"Okay, I'm dialin'!" Jessie exclaimed.

"But Jessie, we just ate like ten pizzas and there's still more left. Just hang up," Bianca insisted.

"*Party pooper,*" Megan teased.

"I think it's my bedtime now," Lexi yawned.

"OMG! I know how to liven up this party! A tried and true classic: Truth or Dare," Bianca said.

Then the room went silent. Who knew what juicy secrets Bianca wanted them to spill?

But Lexi broke the silence with a loud hiccup.

"Good, I have a volunteer to go first!" Bianca exclaimed.

"Uh-oh," Lexi said, crawling under the covers.

"Ballet Ladies, form a circle on the floor, and let's get down to business. Lexi goes first, and then we go clockwise," Bianca told them.

The girls sat in a circle, and giggled together.

"All set, Bee. Go ahead," Jessie nodded.

"Lexi, truth or dare?" Bianca asked.

"Dare," Lexi surprisingly answered.

Then everyone gasped.

"*Dare?* OMG! The baby said dare? Okay, I'll give you a good one," Bianca decided.

"Give it to me," Lexi shot back.

"I dare you to perform the classic Ding 'n Ditch. You have to go next door to Willy's house, ring the doorbell, and run right back without getting caught!" Bianca dared.

"No way!" everyone gasped.

"Piece of cake – I'm outie! Be right back!" Lexi called, disappearing out of the room.

"O-M-G! She's actually going to do it?" Bianca gasped.

"That's one tough little kid," Jessie remarked. "I wouldn't wanna get caught by Billy Bob."

"*Billy Bob?* You mean Willy? That's so funny, Jessie! You're so funny!" Bianca laughed.

"What? But, but, I was gonna say that!" Megan claimed, tugging on Bianca's sleeve.

"Sure you were. C'mon, ladies. Let's watch out the window!" Bianca called, moving the group over to her big window.

They all crowded onto the window seat, and watched little Lexi walk in front of Bianca's house, and straight over to Willy's front porch.

"OMG! She's still wearing her pajamas!" Bianca laughed.

"Cool parachute pants. Not!" Megan laughed.

"They're so big on her! She looks funny!" Jessie laughed.

"She looks like M.C. Hammer!" Bianca called.

"Oh yeah! *Can't touch this! La, la, la, laaa! La, laaa! La, laaa! Hammer time!*" Megan sang, and broke out in her best impression of M.C. Hammer doing the Running Man dance.

"OMG, Megan! You must love VH1 Classic! I bet you watch it all the time!" Bianca laughed.

"But wasn't I funny? Didn't I make you laugh?" Megan panted, slowing down.

"Check it out! The kid's actually ringin' the bell!" Jessie called, pointing out the window.

"Hey, why does Lexi get all the attention?" Megan grumbled, plunking back down on the window seat next to Bianca, and shoving Kaylee to the side.

"Hey, Harry was sitting there!" Kaylee yelled.

"Look, ladies! She just rang the bell! And now she's running back! She actually did it! Run, Lexi! Run!" Bianca cheered, and high-fived Jessie.

A couple minutes later, Lexi came bursting into Bianca's room with a huge smile on her face.

"I did it! I did it! Next dare!" Lexi called, hopping onto Jessie's back and getting a piggy-back ride around Bianca's room.

"Yay Lexi! You're the best at Truth or Dare! You really did it! You're *toe*-tally fabulous!" Bianca praised.

"It's my turn now! Me, me!" Megan yelped.

"So what just happened, Lexi?" Bianca asked, still ignoring Megan.

"Yeah, what happened?" Jessie asked.

"Nobody answered the door. But when I was running back here, Willy yelled out the window to tell Bianca that he's gonna marry her someday," Lexi revealed, giggling.

"*What?*" everyone gasped.

"Oh, that Creepy Willy. Won't he ever stop saying that?" Bianca sighed.

"Well, he does kinda got a big house. Is he really that bad?" Jessie asked.

"Jessie! Yes, he is! He's Creepy Willy! Don't talk like that!" Bianca insisted.

"My turn, my turn!" Megan whined, jumping up and down for attention.

"Fine, Megan. Truth or dare?" Bianca asked.

"I don't know! I can't decide! It's such a big moment! It's my first Truth or Dare with Bianca Best! You tell me what to do!" Megan panicked.

"Goody. Since Lexi already did a dare, you get truth. *Who do you like?*" Bianca asked.

"You mean *like-like?*" Megan asked back.

"Of course I mean like-like! Haven't you played this game before?" Bianca demanded.

"Sure I have! But I don't like-like anyone," Megan claimed.

"What do you mean you don't like-like anyone? Just give me a name! We *are* BFF's, aren't we?" Bianca pushed.

"But I don't know anyone except Willy . . ."

"*Eww! Megan loves Creepy Willy!*" they all sang, teasing Megan.

"Fine, I like Creepy Willy. If that makes me your BFF!" Megan agreed, laughing at herself and turning bright red.

"But Willy's mine!" Kaylee argued.

"OMG!" they all laughed.

Then Lexi started jumping up and down on Bianca's canopy bed.

"No, Lexi! What are you doing? My bed's from France!" Bianca exclaimed.

"*Weeee!*" Lexi squealed, and jumped so high with her arms up in the air, she almost burst through the canopy.

"Whoa! What's gotten into Lil' Lexi?" Jessie asked.

"Chocolate pudding, remember? She ate the whole thing!" Megan laughed.

"Oh yeah! Let's play Truth or Dare all night! This is so much fun! OMG, can you believe we start middle school on Monday?" Bianca asked.

Then everyone went silent and wondered the same thing: would they still be friends in school?

But Bianca broke the silence with:

"Hey, you know we're not just ballet friends. We're *best* friends! I'm not going anywhere!"

"Ooh, ooh, you're not? I mean, of course you're not. But Bianca, you said *we* were best friends! The two of us! Remember?" Megan shrieked.

"Yes Megan, that's true. But I bonded with the other girls, too," Bianca replied.

"But we bonded the most – in the wig closet!" Megan insisted.

"*Wig closet?*" the others shrugged.

"Um, *fig* closet. Megan just loves Fig Newtons," Bianca covered, winking at Megan.

Then Megan smiled, and thought to herself that she really *was* the number one BFF.

"OMG! I think Harry should be our official mascot! He's not exactly a Yorkie, but he'll do for now. You know, Kay, you can't bring a gerbil to middle school," Bianca giggled.

"Okay. I'll keep him in my pocket," Kaylee decided, and turned on Bianca's TV, which was set to VH1 Classic.

Then everyone laughed at Bianca for watching old music videos.

"Hey, let's dance!" Jessie called, doing a pretty *pirouette* in the middle of Bianca's room.

"Nice move!" Bianca cheered, doing a running leap over to Jessie.

And together, the five ballet friends danced and sang along with the music video of Cyndi Lauper's eighties song, "Girls Just Want to Have Fun."

There's more!

Turn the page for a special preview
of the next Ballet Friends book:

#2 Join the Club

Ballet Friends

Join the Club
#2

Chapter One
Beginning

1

bianca's best idea

"Oh Ballet Ladies, are you awake yet? I just got the *best* idea!" Bianca called to her friends, who were snoozing away in their sleeping bags in Bianca's living room.

It was the morning after their first sleepover, and the girls just formed the Ballet Ladies the night before. They even had super cute ballet flats as their official club shoes.

"No, I'm sleeping! Five more minutes?" Megan called back, and made fake snoring sounds.

"Ugg. It's too early," Jessie grumbled, and put her pillow over her head.

"You silly sleepyheads! But I'm a morning person. Isn't anyone gonna get up?" Bianca asked.

"Mommy Bee, I'm awake. Will you braid my hair now?" Lexi asked, skipping over to Bianca who was sitting on the sofa.

"*Mommy Bee?* OMG, I love it! Sit next to me, Lexi. I'd love to braid your hair. Do you want two braids or one big one?" Bianca asked.

"I want lots! Make ten please!" Lexi cheered.

"Ten braids? I don't know if you have enough hair, but I'll try," Bianca said.

"Yay! You're the best at doing hair."

"So you've noticed. But anyway, I'm glad you're up so I can tell you about my super fabulous idea! Guess what we're doing tomorrow?"

"Going to middle school?" Lexi asked.

"Of course, it's our first day of middle school. But what else is gonna happen?" Bianca asked.

"*I'll get lost?*" Lexi guessed.

"Oh Lexi, besides that. It's the activity fair! You know, when we sign up for a school club."

"Oh, sure. I'm signing up for Violin Club! I'm running for President," Lexi boasted.

"Uh, you are? Well, maybe you'll want to do something different? Like form a fabulous ballet club with your new best friends?"

"Huh? But we already made a ballet club. The Ballet Ladies," Lexi stated.

"But I mean a *school* ballet club that we're the founders of! We can meet during activity period, and that way we get an hour together on activity days to hang out and do ballet!" Bianca explained.

"Yay! I wanna hang out with you, Mommy Bee! You're funner than Violin Club!" Lexi cheered.

"Thanks! That means a lot. Do you think the other Ballet Ladies will go for it, too?"

"Um, I think so. Unless Jessie wants to do Basketball Club, and Kay wants to do Greek Club."

"Hmm. Well, I'll definitely get Megan to say yes. Don't you think?" Bianca asked.

"I hope so. But if not, it'll just be the two of us. Because we're best friends!" Lexi exclaimed.

Just then, Megan's BFF radar went off.

"Yikes! Someone turn off the alarm!" she shrieked, shooting out of her sleeping bag with her short red hair sticking straight up.

"Whoa, Megan! What alarm? I don't know what just woke you up, but you can go back to sleep," Bianca replied.

"Huh? Okay," Megan mumbled, going back to sleep.

Then Bianca turned back to Lexi and giggled.

"I love your idea, Mommy Bee! You're gonna make the best Ballet Club President!" Lexi praised.

"And you, the best Ballet Club Vice President!"

"*Reeeally?*" Lexi asked, with her eyes lit up.

"You can be the Vice President of Ballet Buns. How does that sound? That is, if you're not too busy with Violin Club . . ."

"Oh no! You can only sign up for one club, so I'll do Ballet Club with you! I promise!"

"Then it's a deal!" Bianca decided.

"Mommy Bee, what's our club gonna be called?" Lexi asked, while Bianca braided her hair.

"Ballet Club, of course. What a great name, huh?" Bianca giggled.

"Um, I think so," Lexi nodded.

"Oh, we have so much to do tomorrow. We'll need a table at the activity fair, a big, pretty sign that says Ballet Club, an official sign-up sheet, and OMG, I totally forgot! We need a faculty advisor!"

"Oh . . . that sounds too hard. I think I'll do Violin Club. Sorry."

"*What?* But you're the Vice President!" Bianca exclaimed.

"Um, I forgot someone already asked me to do Violin Club and I said yes," Lexi quickly blurted.

"Hey, do you mean that? You know I'll do all the work. Would you think I was weird if I pulled out a Ballet Club poster I made last night when everyone was sleeping?" Bianca revealed.

Then she pulled out something from behind the sofa. It was a big, pink poster with "Ballet Club" written in purple glitter glue.

"Ooh, that's pretty. Purple's my favorite color. Okay, I'll do it! Will you have cookies at our meetings? Violin Club has cookies."

"How do hot and gooey Cinnabons sound? Is that better than Violin Club?" Bianca tempted her.

"Oh boy! That's *way* better than some crummy cookies! When's our first meeting? I'm there!"

Then the founding sisters high-fived.

Made in the USA
Middletown, DE
10 February 2019